Praise for *The J...*

"A rare treat to find characters we can care about this much."  —*Philadelphia Inquirer*

"As authentic as sand in one's shoes."  —Edward Hoagland

"The book is a prism of loneliness in the form of a novel."  —*Los Angeles Times*

"Drawing on pioneer diaries, journals, and hand-me-down stories of her own ancestors, Gloss displays a deep awareness not only of the brutal hardships of frontier life, but also of the moral codes and emotional attachments of the people who settled there."  —*Publishers Weekly*

"There is a gentle, touching overcast to this raw-knuckled pioneer story of a lone (but, she insists, not '"lonely"') hardship-honed widow homesteading in 1895 Oregon.... Gloss's conscientious McPhee-like detailing of hand-blistering homesteading toil is achingly effective; but it's the author's reading of lives locked in by hardship, loneliness, and real danger, and of their careful steps toward community, that is so appealing."  —*Kirkus Reviews*

"A powerful novel of struggle and loss."  —*Dallas Morning News*

"Every gritty line of the story rings true ... extraordinarily fine writing."  —*Seattle Times*

# The
# Jump-Off
# Creek

Books by Molly Gloss

*Unforeseen: Stories*
*Falling from Horses*
*The Hearts of Horses*
*Wild Life*
*The Dazzle of Day*
*The Jump-Off Creek*
*Outside the Gates*

# The Jump-Off Creek

## A Novel

• • •

# MOLLY GLOSS

HARPER ● PERENNIAL

NEW YORK • LONDON • TORONTO • SYDNEY • NEW DELHI • AUCKLAND

HARPER ● PERENNIAL

A hardcover edition of this book was published in 1989 by Houghton Mifflin Company.

FIRST HOUGHTON MIFFLIN PAPERBACK PUBLISHED IN 1990.
FIRST MARINER BOOKS EDITION PUBLISHED IN 1999.
REPRINTED BY HARPER PERENNIAL IN 2024.

The Library of Congress has catalogued the previous edition of this book as follows:

Gloss, Molly.
The jump-off creek / Molly Gloss.
    p.   cm.
ISBN 0–395–51086–4
ISBN 0–618–56587–6 (pbk).
I. Title.
PS3557.L65J8                                                      1989
813'.54—dc20 89–32157 CIP

ISBN 978-0-618-56587-0 (pbk.)

HB 09.27.2024

*For My Great-Grandmothers—*

*Molly Mizell Donaldson*
1875–1944, Miles, Texas

*Emma Castle Hurlburt Bettey*
1862–1924, Walla Walla, Washington

*Nancy Kerr Lovelace*
1853–1938, Irion County, Texas

*Lena Meyers Remlinger*
1860–1930, Fort Vancouver, Washington

*—Westering Women, All*

I am greatly indebted to many published and unpublished diaries, letters and journals of women who settled the West. I hope their strong, honest voices can be heard in this book.

I'm grateful to Tony Wolk and Dee Anne Westbrook, who read the manuscript with care and perception; and to Ed, who gave me time, encouragement, applause.

I must also thank my dad, who introduced me to the public library, and to the panorama of the real and imagined West.

# The
# Jump-Off
# Creek

## ❊ 1 ❊

*6 April* Bought the black hinny Mule today, $18, also the spavint gray as my money is so short and I have hope he will put on wt, his eyes are clear w a smart look in them and his feet not tender. Believe I am now outfitted, shall start out at Day Break. Weather is poor w rain & a cold wind, not a favorable day for travel but I shall not put it off, each days boarding $3 I can ill afford and now the stables cost of 2 Mules & the Goats. My list of needs has many unhappy lines drawn through marking out this or that not so nec at prices so very dear. O well the poor Mules will be hard put to carry the things as is. I have stld my accts w Mrs Mailer as I plan to be gone in the morning before she is about. She has given me a good rolling pin from her own kitchen as well as many candle stubs & ends of wax, tho not in other ways been over kind these few days I have boarded. I believe she thinks I am a Mad Woman or worse. For myself, after so long in getting to this day, I find I am not much afraid — but in that may be some proof of my Madness. I shall not see Mrs Mailer nor perhaps any woman, at least until the Fall if I am still alive then and able to come out for my Winter's nec. But I am used to being Alone, in spirit if not in body, and shall *not* be Lonely, as I never have been inclined that way. I believe what I feel is just a keenness to get to that place and stand under my own roof at last.

# ❖ 2 ❖

At the head of Buck's Creek where the springs puddled out to fill the low ground, sometimes there would be as many as half a dozen cows standing along the edges of the pond, tearing at the grass. But there weren't any there now, only old, sucking tracks in the mud, from yesterday or the day before. In a fine silent rain, Tim rode once around the pond and then went down from there, scouting the blind gullies where snow-melt fed down toward the Buck's. He was half a day before he finally turned up three cows sharing the skimpy grass with their calves, up one of the dead-end canyons.

He let the dog do most of the work. He hung back, holding a short loop of rope open against his thigh, while the dog broke the cows out gently toward the creek. The left-behind calves bawled a little for their mamas and jig-trotted after them, but shortly the cows settled into a walk and the calves sorted out which mother was which and nuzzled flanks with fitful, bawling complaint. Tim and the dog shunted back and forth behind them, keeping them headed right without seeming to do much. Tim's breath was white, thinning around his shoulders as he rode through it.

Where an old lightning strike had burned a clearing, he called up the dog and let the cows nose the wet grass and weeds growing among the snags on both sides of the creek. Then he stood off the horse and squatted to kindle a little fire behind a windbreak of wood. The trees had not seemed much of a shelter, but now on the bare slope the rain came down harder. He pulled inside his oilskin as far as he could get and made a wordless sound of annoyance. At the little noise, the dog came and squatted next to him and Tim opened his palms.

"Hey," he said, in a low voice. When the dog pushed his face against his hands, Tim ruffled the dog's wet coat.

He put coffee and beans to heat and hunched on the damp grass, waiting for it, looking out at the cows. Once, aloud, he said, "Three goddamn calves." The dog looked toward him then but without much interest, hearing no temper in it, just a dull grayness like the rain.

Tim drank coffee from the spigot of his pot, sucking it down gingerly. Then he ate beans with a dipper of hard bread and put the pan on the grass for the dog to finish while he tightened the saddle. Behind him, he heard the pan bump a few times and then the dog's low warning. He didn't look around yet. He dropped the fender of the saddle and stepped unhurriedly around the backside of the horse.

He didn't know the woman who came toward him from the edge of the burnt clearing. She sat high and straight on a big black mule, towing behind her another mule that looked thin-necked, ribby, with a spavined hock. There was gear hanging everywhere off her high-cantled saddle, and off the heaped-up load on the other, the gray mule. She had, besides, two filthy goats on a long tether.

She pulled up the saddle mule when she was still a little way from Tim. "How do you do," she said, gravely polite, and in a moment, smiling in a flat way, "I smelled your campfire smoke."

There was a short silence before it occurred to him: "Coffee is still hot," he said, ducking his chin, and he went back around the horse to the fire and the blackened pot. She sat a minute, watching him, and then she swung a leg across and stood down stiffly beside the mule. She had kilted her skirt up so she could ride astride, bringing the back hem up between her legs and tucking it into the front of her waistband. Without busyness, she pulled the skirt free, shook it out, smoothed it with the palms of her hands. The coat she had on was too big, mouse-colored, the collar standing up high around her neck. She looked pipe-thin inside it, her arms thin as sticks where they stuck out of the folded-up sleeves, her face thin too, but for a big chin, a wide straight mouth. In the shadow beneath a floppy man's hat, her skin looked coarse, he could see the set-in creases by her mouth and between her brows.

He reached the pot to her handle-backward. "I've got no cup," he said, not quite looking at her.

She seemed not to care. She came across the little distance to him, took the pot solemnly and tested the spigot against her mouth. It was bitter coffee, but she drank it without making any face. When she had taken a few swallows she gave him a stiff smile over the edge of the pot. "Good," she said.

He looked around him for something else to offer her. "Beans are eaten up," he said. "But there's bread."

She made a slight refusing motion with her head while she kept drinking the coffee. Then she let the pot down and said, "Hot coffee is all I hoped for. It has proved to be a cold day." She stood holding the pot in her two hands, cupping her palms tenderly around the blackened, beat-up tin. She had long thin fingers. He could see the nails were all bitten down or broken, the skin around them tough and thickened.

In a moment, unexpectedly, she let go the coffeepot with one hand and held out her arm toward him. "I am Lydia Bennett Sanderson."

He had put both his own hands in his pockets to keep them anchored, and now he fumbled, pulling them out so he could shake. "Tim Whiteaker," he said. He let go her hand and stood back from her. In a moment, silently, she handed over the emptied coffeepot, offering with it another of her little smiles. He occupied himself, dumping out his thrice-used grounds and stowing both his pots in the kit behind his saddle. When he turned again, she was standing over his bit of a fire with both her sooty palms held open to the flames.

He waited through a long silence while she stood that way, disregarding him. Finally, carefully, he said, "You're a good way off the beaten track, ma'am."

She looked toward him and blinked solemnly and the rain went off her eyelashes. The look in her face became stiff again. He could see her eyes were tearless.

"I have bought a place along the Jump-Off Creek," she said, and swung one hand in a vague gesture east or north or both.

He was not much surprised. Once in Montana and a couple of times later in the Spokane country, he had known women who'd homesteaded alone. They had had a steadfast look, or a doggedness, and now that he was watching for it, he could see it in this woman's face. He thought what he had taken for thinness might be a hard, worn-down lean.

"You're a way from the Jump-Off too, if you don't mind my saying so, ma'am."

She tightened in her wide mouth like it was a drawstring purse, little creases raying out around it, but then right away let go that look, let her mouth out flat again like he hadn't hit any sore place at all. "I believe the advice I got was not good."

"Which way did you come, ma'am?"

"I left La Grande yesterday and Summerville this morning, taking the Thomas and Ruckel Road."

"There is a trail that spurs off that road shortly after the forks of the Thomas Creek, and that would get you over to the Jump-Off after a while."

Her mouth stayed flat. "Yes. I was told so."

Tim ducked his head, looking away from her out to the cows and then down to the dog. "I haven't gone out to that road myself in a while. I guess that trail isn't much used, nor the road either, since the railroad has been put through."

"No," she said. "I don't believe it has been kept up." He thought he could hear the little pique in it, as if he might be to blame for that, and he felt something like irritation himself. It wasn't him that was lost.

He scuffed his boot, pushing mud up over the fire. The woman stood back from the smoke. "If you go south from here, in a while you'll come out on the Oberfield Ranch Road. It isn't much of a road, but you'll see the wagon marks in the mud." He didn't quite look at her. He kept kicking at the last of the fire. "East on the Oberfield Road will get you on back to the Ruckel so you can try again. There's a dead old yew tree about where your trail is, and if you get to the place where the roadbed is washed out on the left side, you're past it by about a mile."

He caught up the bay's reins and whistled to the dog without ever plainly looking at the woman. Then he touched his hat brim with his hand, said, "Good luck to you, ma'am," and toed the stirrup, allowing the horse to move away, hop-trotting, before he had settled in the saddle.

He thought she might call to him. But as he and dog gathered in the cattle, he could see her there beside the faint scarf of smoke, dividing her skirt again and then pulling at the knots on those mules and retying them. She looked toward him once with a level, indifferent glance, and in a moment deliberately away. *Hell with it then*, he thought. But from the far edge of the trees, in the gray drizzle, there was no seeing her prickly look, there was just the thin, solitary woman-shape of her in that big old coat. And finally, with a grumbled sound that made the dog look, Tim reined the horse back toward her.

He didn't come all the way back. From a little distance, holding the bay's head up, he called out to her. "From here, I guess you'd be quicker following the Buck's Creek on down to where it runs into the North Fork. From there it's plain, and a short way to the Jump-Off."

She stood looking at him, not speaking, just hunching her shoulders to pull her hands up inside her coat sleeves so she looked like a cat that was mad, or a humpback. *Suit yourself*, he thought. But in a bit he gestured with one hand toward the creek that ran downhill across the burnt clearing. "There's no trail to speak of beside most of the Buck's. We just follow the ridge as best we can. I'm running these cows down that way. If you wanted, you could follow us up."

Then finally she bent her head, looking at her boots or maybe nodding. She was solemn, no stiff little edge of smile showing this time. He didn't say more. He touched his hat again and turned back to the cows. In a while, from the shadow under the edge of the trees, he looked back. At a deliberate distance the woman followed, sitting up straight-backed and unsmiling on her mule, and trailing behind her that tomfoolish little string of goats, and the skinny mule.

The cows found their separate ways through the trees, not hurrying. Tim let them go pretty nearly as they would, so long as they kept to the ridge or the sidehill above the line of the creek. It had been raining most of the week and every little crease in the ridge carried water in a brown spurt. The cows waded the rills or skirted around the gullies, depending on their humor. Tim rode hunched and heavy, watching the dog. Once or twice he looked back toward the woman, not coming all the way around, just twisting neck to peer briefly at her from below the edge of his hat. She let the mule choose a way without following his bay horse exactly. She looked solemn, her big mouth flat. Inside the mouse-colored coat she was stiff as a larch pole.

He had come up this way early in the day, with the horse worming sideways on the sloppy grass crossing the treeless shoulder of the Dutchman's Ridge. Now when he got up there the whole side of the ridge was gone in a great brown chute. The cows came up to the edge of the slide and stood about dully in the rain. Tim sat on his horse behind them, staring at the slide, while the dog waited for him to make up his mind.

When the woman's mule brought her slowly out of the trees, he said, without looking toward her, "We ought to go down, I guess." But then, ducking his chin, he did look at her. "You might want to walk down, ma'am, or let me lead that mule. He's liable to slip in this wet."

She looked down the steep side of the hill to the creek, and then brought her eyes around to him, making that crabbed face, drawing her mouth in and letting it out. He couldn't tell if it was for him or for that steep trail. "He's very steady, Mr. Whiteaker." She said it in a sure way, speaking his name carefully as if it were two words — White, Acre.

He hunched his shoulders. In a bit he said, "Suit yourself, ma'am."

She set her mouth and then jigged the mule straight downhill, not waiting at all, just taking a tighter hold of the leads and going down. She stood in the stirrups so her weight was out over the saddle-mule's hindquarters, and the mule picked a careful path, swaggering low on his haunches, bracing stiff forelegs in a mincing jolty gait. The goats didn't mind going down, but the gray mule rolled its eyes white and hung back at the taut end of its lead, sliding down awkwardly on its bunch-muscled butt. Tim sat where he was and watched them. When she rode the mule into the creek in a last rattling slide of rock and mud, he heard her little whoop, but he couldn't tell whether it was scare or jubilation.

Stubbornly, he took his own advice. He started the cows, the horse, the yellow dog scrambling down sloppily ahead of him, following the muddy slide mark of the woman's gray mule, and he came down slowly on foot, stepping carefully in his high-heeled boots, skidding, braced on his hands the last little way when his feet went out from under him. She sat at the bottom of the gully among the jumble of animals, waiting. There was some pink in her face.

He stood at the edge of the creek, not looking toward her, while he pushed his hair back up under his hat with the heel of one dirty hand. Then he gave the dog the word, took hold of the bay's reins and started off afoot, finding a rough way along the creekbank with the windfalls spanning the narrow gully like jackstraws. After a while he slid a look back after the woman. She followed him, leading the mule, walking, with that solemn look she had. She watched where she stepped. The edge of her dank skirt flapped around her boots.

The cows went around a few snags but then came up against one with no way around, and they stood along it and faced the dog contrarily. Tim had to lift the calves over and then prod the cows to clamber over after them, throwing his arms out jerkily, whistling shrill through his teeth. When they had got over, he looked back at the woman once, cautiously. But he didn't wait for her. She might have been glad enough for it, bunching up her big skirt in her hands, showing black muddy stockings when she swung her boots over.

The high place named Bear's Camp Mountain was a long turned-back ridge, not much more than that, with a lot of narrow brushy folds running down from it, good places to hide if you were a cow. Going up there, Blue spooked a bunch of horses and ran with them a way until he saw they were Carroll Oberfield's, then he pulled up and whistled back the dog and rode on up the grassy shoulder of the mountain. In the gray dampness there wasn't much sound, just the squeak of leather, the soft placing of the horse's feet. The dog trotted silently, mouth shut, coat full out against the chill. Blue wriggled his feet sometimes in the thin worn boots. His toes were damp, cold.

Sometimes they cut sign, day-old pies or muddy slurred prints, but there wasn't anything clear enough, fresh enough to follow. They crosshatched the mountain, working slowly down to the spring.

He nooned at the spring, squatting on his haunches behind a tiny blaze, smoking a cigarette while a can of corn heated. He held the cigarette with his left hand, letting the right one rest against his doubled-up leg. His collarbone ached. The dog lay flat on his belly near him, watching him while he smoked and then while he ate, and coming in quick for the leftovers when he stood to scuff out the coals. Blue, waiting for the dog, shrugged his shoulders to try to loosen the bunched-up muscles at the base of his neck.

There was a little warning, a racketing noise like a breaking of limbs, and then a big steer cleared the rise in front of him, eyeing whitely down the steepness of its face and then pivoting to go along the backbone, running loplegged, clumsy. Blue was reaching for the bridle of his horse when the rifle reported through the sodden trees and the steer missed a step and went over, shoulder first, skidding up a comber of mud and pine needles. Before the steer had stopped good, a man burst through the trees along his backtrail, riding hard-trot on a little buckskin horse, holding a carbine high in his right hand. He was looking after the steer but he must have seen Blue there from an edge of his eye. His face jerked, showing pale twist of surprise and alarm. He yanked the buckskin around, slobbering, clanking the bit, and as he jabbed his spurs to send the horse back out of sight, Blue was grabbing at the roan, kicking past the dog to vault for his saddle. The dog made an offended, yowling sound, but by then Blue had booted the roan and was sailing the muddy water of the spring. The horse took the far slope in half a dozen grunting jumps. They cleared the steer's carcass at the top of the ridge and started down through the trees after the buckskin. It wasn't steep. He felt the roan's off front leg skip cadence, that was all, then the flash of trees in a high wheeling spin.

The rain came very meekly out of a low oyster-colored sky. For a while he lay where he was, in the rain, waiting for his breath. The dog came and smelled him and touched the back of his hand with his wet nose and then squatted to wait.

*All right,* he thought. *Get up.*

He took hold of his right shoulder with his left hand and rolled up to a sit. He began to sweat softly beneath the dampness of his clothes. When he had sat a while, he brought his legs under and came to a wobbly stand. He was still holding on to his shoulder. He'd broken the collarbone twice before. But under the squeeze of his hand, there was a bright ache, no scrape of bone, nothing grinding. Maybe it was okay this time, or would be. In a moment, blood dribbled from one of his eyebrows and ran down his cheek. He touched his face timidly, found a sticky wound above one eye. *Shit.*

He turned his head carefully, looking along the scarred slope where the roan, spilling, had raked a long gouge through the duff. The horse was waiting, standing patient, watching him. He limped down through the scrub to where the horse stood. "Jay," he said, stroking the velvet muzzle once in apology. Then he squatted and ran his palm over the horse, each muddy leg in turn, then the ribs and chest, the shoulders. The roan's wet shag fell out in hanks in his hand.

Above him on the ridge, the dead steer lay in a skid of wet leaves. Blue stood resting his forehead against the horse's neck. He thought of letting the steer lay up there, letting the coyotes have it. Then he grunted sourly and went up the ridge, knelt in the wet and unfolded his knife.

*Shit.* "Shit," he said, and the dog, hearing aggravation, turned his eyes away under raised-up, anxious brows.

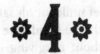

They had come up gradually on the ridge. There was a line of pines along the creek but finally they could look across the tips of them, and when they came out of the timber Lydia saw the trail ahead of Mr. Whiteaker was a little rocky line chased on the steep treeless face of the slope.

Mr. Whiteaker waited, as he had only done the one other time, above the mud slide, judging the steep downhill. He looped one of his legs around the saddle horn and massaged the knee carefully, sliding his hand up under the edge of the stiff oilskin. He did not look back toward her. He watched the dog persuading the cows single file ahead of him along the narrow track in the bluff. She watched the dog herself. Until seeing this one, she had not ever seen a dog do a true job of work, only Lars's foolish retriever bringing up a dead barn swallow or a hatchling quail from the stubble of the barley field, carrying the bird clamped between his jaws and then letting it down happily in the yard. Mr. Whiteaker's dog was big-headed, mud yellow, ugly. There was a hitch in his gait, an old or a false limp. But she liked to watch his steady, inconspicuous effort, keeping the cows together and headed right.

When the mule had brought her up to him, Mr. Whiteaker dropped his leg down in a stiff way and toed the stirrup. He sat hunched under his oilskin, looking off vaguely into the trees behind her. "Some people get a dread of high places," he said in a low voice. He had a gesture, ducking his chin like a horse trying to get loose of the rein, and he did that now. She could not tell, yet, whether it was a habit of discomfort or of temper. "I knew a cowboy once who wouldn't ride a horse that stood more than fifteen hands. He said he started to sweat if he got any higher than that."

She made a thin, brief smile for his sake, and pinched the collar of Lars's coat tight with one hand. She had been up on the roof of her dad's barn without misgiving, that was about her only experience with highness. She would not say that, if she could keep from it.

He ducked his chin again, shifted his weight. "If you think you would want both hands, ma'am, I'll hang onto your string for you." He said it in a low way, glancing aside: she saw in his face that he was wary of her.

She had not ever found just the right manner for these occasions. She smiled carefully, looking past him along the narrow notch of the trail. "I have never had any fear of highness myself, Mr. Whiteaker," she said.

His shoulders moved slightly inside his dirty corduroy coat. "All right then," he said. He turned and nudged the bay down the little notch, and the mule went behind him without pressing.

Away from the trees, the wind drove the rain ahead of it. Lydia pulled her hat down on her ears, hunched her shoulders inside the collar edge of the coat. She looked down once toward the distant pencil stroke of the creek and after that kept her eyes on a place just in front of the mule's stride, watching the puddles that riffled cold and brown in the wind.

"Okay, ma'am?" Mr. Whiteaker had hipped around on the saddle to look back at her. His shout sounded reedy, thin. She nodded once and smiled in a bare way and he turned frontward again, settling his shoulders against the wind and the rain. Ahead of him the cattle went along quick, anxious, pussy-footing. They had, maybe, a dread of high places. She held her mouth and looked fixedly past them, where the trail went steeply down across the face of the ridge and finally under the trees.

The mule jerked his head suddenly, but it was Mr. Whiteaker who shouted, whatever word or name it was blown thin on the weather. She looked and saw him put one hand on the neck of the bay horse, and the bay wallowing under him as if his touch had done that. Her heart pitched too: she heard or felt the little sideslip of gravel. He yelled again, maybe at the horse, and the bay shoved ahead, bunching his big hindquarters in a grunting lunge. The edge of the trail slumped under him, but he was already down the notch, jumping ahead in a jolty high canter, when the rocks scrambled loose down the long bluff. The mule flung up his head, backsquatting as though he wanted to sit. Lydia put her hand flat on his jerking neck and held him steady. Three or four feet were gone out of the trail. The broken edge was stubbled, rocky. She looked at it.

Mr. Whiteaker called something to her, she could not hear what it was, and he swung down to loosen the cinch on his horse. She saw him stand holding on to the saddle a moment before he let go and worked the buckles. The bay stood for him restlessly, rolling the bit, huffing air. There was a shallow cut along the shank of the horse's off rear leg. Mr. Whiteaker wet his neckerchief in the rill along the notch and daubed away the gritty mud and blood. She sat stiffly on the mule, in the gusty rain, and watched him.

Finally he came back up the trail to the broken edge. A little color had bloomed in his face. "Give those goats a swat. See if they won't jump across," he said to her.

She had one hand twined tight around the saddle horn, the fingers holding on rubbery. She thought of backing her way off the hillside. *I believe I'll just go around, thank you.* And he would take his cows and go on without waiting. *Suit yourself, ma'am.*

But she stood down from the mule, careful and grim, and pulled the goats up on the long tether. She remembered suddenly that one of the does was named Rose; the man who had owned her had called her after his wife's mother. She didn't know the name of the other goat, nor which of them was Rose. She stood, fishing uselessly for the name. Louise. The brown doe was Louise, after the man's own mother. She undid the lead and bunched it up in a coat pocket. Then, standing at the edge of the short gravelly slide where the trail had broken down, she slapped Rose's flank smartly. The goat shied, twitched her hide, blatted. Lydia got behind her and slapped again and pushed on her hindquarters. Rose made a cross sound gathering herself, and shot across the break. Louise bolted after her, stuttering and bleating protest at the edge.

Mr. Whiteaker had got back out of the way, squatting up on the steep sidehill. Now he stood up. "If you'll sling me the end of the pack mule's lead, I'll see if I can persuade him to come over."

The wind flapped the brim of his hat suddenly and he jerked his arm up, holding onto it. She held her own hat and waited until the gusty wind had fallen off. Then silently she brought the gray mule up and cast the lead across to Mr. Whiteaker. He pulled it and made a wordless, foolish clucking sound. The mule stood stubbornly with his neck stretched out, eyeing whitely over the edge of the trail down to the pine trees and the creek. Lydia slapped his haunch.

"If you've got a stick, ma'am, hit him with it."

She had no stick. She backed up from the mule and threw a rock. It smacked him at the root of the tail and he jerked and came over in a clumsy bounce, jolting his top-heavy load. The man let go the lead, let him go on by, trotting high-headed down the notch to take comfort from the bay horse and the goats, bunched up together halfway down to the trees.

"Now you, ma'am," he said. He ducked his chin. "I don't know if you want to jump that mule over, or get over on your own."

She had got to recognize in the faces of most cattlemen a little conceit about mules. She had seen it once, maybe, in Mr. Whiteaker's face, but there was nothing of it now, just that slight wariness.

She stood beside the black saddle mule, in the rain, and looked ahead along the notch, not at him. "This mule has not even a name yet, Mr. Whiteaker, I have not known him long enough for that." She glanced toward him. "But I have a general trust of mules on tricky ground."

He stood holding on to his hat, squinting at her through the rain. Then he said, in a low way, "I believe if you give him your heels, he'll bring you across okay, ma'am."

She nodded gravely and got up on the mule. She had a habit of going quick in these events, before the misgiving would set in. She gripped the horn, made a little involuntary squeaky sound, rammed her heels against the mule. The mule squatted back, deciding, and then they came over in a clumsy leap. Her bottom rose off the saddle and slapped down when they lit on the other side. She let the mule take her on downslope at a jittery trot, straight on past the bunched-up animals. They fell in after her, as if she had them on a lead. Even the bay horse started down, jerking his head, fretting.

When she came down under the trees, she got stiffly off the mule and stood there. The dog had brought Mr. Whiteaker's cattle down onto the flatter ground and he was holding them patiently, waiting. He came and smelled Lydia where she was standing beside the mule. When she saw Mr. Whiteaker coming down on the trail, she took the lead out of her pocket and looked at the goats and then went after them slowly.

The shank of the bay horse dribbled a little blood through muddy hair. The man, when he came down, squatted looking at that without speaking to her. The horse made a low, snuffling sound when he touched the leg. He straightened up and reached under the saddle, tightening the rigging. "We'd have been quite a while, taking any other way down off that ridge," he said. She understood that it was a kind of apology.

She nodded, with her mouth deliberately unsmiling. "Well, we have got down all right," she said.

He looked at her. "Yes."

The horse stamped its foot.

"I have been told that a solution of carbolic will keep the corruption out of a wound," she said, while he bent down looking at the sore leg again.

He glanced around at her. After a silence, he said, "I don't know if I have any of it. I guess we ought to get some." He nodded as if she had said something more. Then he stood and climbed up on the saddle and said a word to his dog. He started to follow the cows. But then she saw him straighten suddenly and he stopped his horse and got down again and left the horse standing there while he went up the steep side of the hill beside the trail. The dog came a short way with him and then made a sound, a vague throaty gnarl, and squatted to wait. On the wind, suddenly, Lydia had a breath of something rank. She saw what Mr. Whiteaker was after, the dead steer lying flat along the brushy hillside. Some of the belly had been eaten out and a hindquarter was gone, gnawed or cut away. A fox was dead on the grass too, a young thin one tongue-choked and staring, and a pair of blue-black ravens, feathers standing askew on the wind.

Mr. Whiteaker pushed against the carcass with his boot. Then he walked all the way around it slowly, expressionlessly, not puckering his face against the smell. He stepped over the ravens, out around the fox pup, then came back down the little slope to where she and the dog waited. He might have gone on without a word, but she said, "Mr. Whiteaker?" so that it was a question, and that made him stand a minute.

He looked across at her and then back toward the dead animals and then, tiredly, he began to rub his eyes with the knuckles of his forefingers, twisting them both together, back and forth in little half circles the way a child would. There were pairs of long curving creases beside his mouth and his eyes, and she thought suddenly: they gave him the look of a little boy tickled and not liking it, a sort of pained, unwilling smile.

"Times are hard," he said, blinking, dropping his hands. "A wolf gets eastern money for the pelt, and the state is paying a bounty for the ears. So I guess half the cowboys on the grub line have got poison in their kits. If nothing else presents itself, some of them will bait up a cow. Sometimes it's not wolf that eats the bad meat." He didn't look toward her, nor toward the carcasses. He looked down along the gully where his cows were wandering off, lowering their big heads to the tufts of grass.

"In the La Grande paper this week or last, I believe I saw the wolf bounty was to be done away with," she said.

He looked at her in surprise. "Is that right?" Then he ducked his head. "I worked in Montana when I was a kid, twenty years ago when there was still buffalo. The wolfers would bait with buffalo over there. I knew a man brought in two hundred pair of ears from a winter's work. But that was a long time ago. There's a hell of a lot more work to it now, and a hell of a lot less sense. A one-loop outfit is liable to lose more cows to wolfer than ever went to timber wolf." He gave her a quick look afterward, so that she saw boyishness in his face again: it was the look boys have when they begin to swear, their eyes shying around to see what effect it has. "Pardon, ma'am," he said, muttering and looking away from her.

She said solemnly, "That's all right, Mr. Whiteaker."

In a while Buck's Creek ran down into some other water. Mr. Whiteaker stopped his horse and named the creek — "This is the North Fork of the Meacham," he said. There was a good beaten trail along it. A spurt of water ran in every crosswise channel and spilled across the track in a slippery thin sheet, but she thought a careful mule wagon might get through along that trail in summer when the mud had gone dry and hard. Probably the downstream end of it came out at the rail line along the Meacham Creek.

He gestured with his head. "Upstream from here, ma'am, the next gully with more than a little piddly runoff in it will be the Jump-Off. There is a trail goes up there."

She looked upstream, nodding.

"You know where you're going from there?" he said.

She looked toward him. He had been careful, had not said, *I don't suppose you can get lost from here.*

"I have bought the deed to Mr. Claud Angell's land," she said. She ought to have got the way from someone besides the real estate man, gone up one of the narrow rutted lanes off the Ruckel Road there above Summerville and asked at a farm door — *Do you know the Claud Angell place?* They'd have known the Jump-

Off Creek, anyway, and she'd have been able to find it out from there without going about lost in the wet trees and playing The Damfool Woman for this Mr. Whiteaker.

He nodded as if he was not surprised. It may have been that Angell's was the only house on the Jump-Off. He dismounted his horse and walked on the rocks, leading the bay out until the water came up white around the horse's legs. He pushed up one sleeve and squatted to wash out the little cut along the bay's shank. Then he straightened again, lifted his hat, combed his wet fingers back through his hair. She saw a high forehead, white above the line of hat shadow. Looking at her sideways, he said, "Angell, he never had much of a place."

She made a small deliberate smile. "No. I was told so."

He pulled down his damp sleeve and looked at her again, glancing, uncomfortable. "He never did farm that land. He used to cut ties for the railroad and when the line was put through he ran a few cattle."

She nodded. "Yes. I mean to raise cattle myself."

He glanced at the goats. "I figured you would be wanting to farm," he said, low.

She shook her head. "No. Or only so much as will keep me from starvation." She smiled slightly.

He led the bay out of the water and stood a moment fiddling with his saddle, smoothing the webbing where it pulled through the rings. He didn't look toward her. Finally he said, "Last time I went by there, a couple of cowboys was squatted in Angell's shack." He glanced toward her across the dip of the saddle. "Maybe they've moved on by now."

She sat still on the mule, taking it in. In a while she said, "I have a clear deed." She said it as flat as might be.

He looked at her but he didn't say any more about Angell or the squatters. He just nodded once, slowly, and climbed up on the horse. He looked graceless, clumsy, swinging up his stiff leather chaps.

"Where is your own place, Mr. Whiteaker?"

He gestured vaguely down the North Fork of the Meacham. "We dammed up the springs of the Chimney Creek for a pond." He seemed to think something over. Then he said, "There's only four or five lived-in houses between the Ruckel Road and Meacham Creek. We're your next neighbor, I guess."

He had an unmistakable bachelor's look, hair hanging shaggy, the collar edge of his shirt black with old stain. She said, without hope, "You don't have a family, Mr. Whiteaker."

He dipped his chin. "No. There's me and Blue, we are neither one of us married." Then he said, "We have got about thirteen hundred acres between the two of us," so that it became clear it was not the dog who was named Blue. A partner.

"You aren't farming."

"No. Cattle." He looked at her. "We've been picking up some of Angell's cows with ours. When you get time, you can come over and take them home."

The country was rough and steep, probably everybody's cattle ran together, there would be little help for it with the way the land lay. But it seemed plain that if Claud Angell had stayed gone and no one had come to claim his place, Mr. Whiteaker and his partner would have put their own brand on the Angell calves.

She said, nodding her head once, "Thank you. I appreciate your holding on to them."

He nodded too. "Yes, ma'am." He put his hat on, touched his fingers to the brim. "Good luck." He started his horse, following the dog and the cows down the wide trail.

"Thank you, Mr. Whiteaker."

He looked back across his shoulder without stopping the horse, only ducking his chin or nodding once, she couldn't tell which. "Welcome, ma'am." He settled back around and went on.

Lydia thumped her heels against the mule and pulled his head around hard to get him to go up the North Fork. He wanted to follow the bay horse.

The rain had not quit. Her back ached from riding hunch-shouldered with the collar of Lars's coat turned up around her cold neck. She had cold feet too, the boots poor to start with, too big, filled out with newspaper. But she had not ever found much reward for woefulness. She tightened her mouth, raising a familiar little buttress against misery. She made a plan, several plans, for handling whomever might be found in Claud Angell's house, supposing the difficulties one after the other and answering them in a dogged way.

The shack sat in a stumpy clearing more or less on the flat, with the Jump-Off Creek going slow through the weeds past the front of the house. It was built with unskinned pine logs chinked poorly with mud and fern and moss. The house was eight feet by twelve, no more than that, listing slightly to the south. There was an open-face leanto, like a hat brim, at one end of the building inside a half circle of failing brush fence. Two horses stood under it, looking dismal and uncomforted.

Lydia sat on the mule. She held her shoulders up straight. "Hello," she said, calling it out loud. The creek made little noise running slow across the flat of the clearing, so she heard the surprise from inside the shack, the knock of a boot against a wall, or chair legs against a board floor. In a moment a boy came out through the door, swinging it back on tin can hinges until its edge caught in mud. He was combing his hair with the fingers of both hands, blinking and squinting against the gray dusk. Behind him the room looked dark; she saw the floor was dirt.

"How do you do," she said, without getting down from the mule.

The boy looked at her. He was sixteen or seventeen. There was a thin, pale mustache trying to grow across his upper lip. His hair stuck up in a cowlick along the front where his fingers hadn't gotten it to lie flat.

"Ma'am," he said finally, looking past her and then back to her in something like confusion. Another boy came and stood next to him, just out of the doorway. He was not much older, maybe twenty. He had put on his hat, or had never taken it off. Under the shadow of the brim she could see his mustache had had time to grow in full and brown, drooping long at the corners of his mouth. They both stood and looked at her.

"Do you know, is this the Claud Angell place?" she said. She knew it was. The trees that had been cleared out for acres around it had surely gone to make ties for the railroad.

The younger one pulled up his shoulders in a sort of shrug. "We heard it was. Hasn't been anybody living here in a while, though." He lifted one hand, swinging it vaguely. "We're just camped," he said, and looked sideways at his friend.

"Wasn't anybody living here," the older one said, in a low, self-conscious mutter.

She became unexpectedly, unreasonably embarrassed. She looked away from them. *I have a clear deed,* she had said to Tim Whiteaker, but could not get those words out now. "I have taken up Mr. Angell's claim, if this is his," she said finally, gently.

They stood looking at her. After a while the younger one shifted his feet. "We were just camping," he said. "We're headed over for Pendleton, we heard there was an outfit over there that was hiring." He looked at the other boy.

There was a silence. Then the older one, in his low voice, said, "We was about to eat. We'd share it, if you want. It ain't much, though." He put both his hands in his pockets and looked past her. In the fine rain, under the darkening sky, his face looked smooth and pale, childlike.

"Thank you. I have been all day without eating at all."

She stood down from the saddle and shook her skirt out while they watched her. She looked at the goats, the mules, and then left them standing, leads trailing among the squatty stumps, and went through the door between the two silent boys who stood framing it. There was a single room, floorless and dark and bare. In it was a little monkey stove, rusted through along its bottom edge, a one-legged bunk balanced in a corner, a three-legged table, a wooden box nailed to the wall beside the stove. The floor was muddy, puddled where the roof leaked. There were sawn-open tin cans and drifts of spent coffee grounds in the front corner near the stove, saddles and chaps and kit bags piled up along a wall. The whole place had a dank and fetid smell — mouse droppings and decayed garbage and rotted wood.

The two of them came in behind her. The younger one fussed around with the stove, feeding in broken limbs and poking at the flames without looking toward her. The older one lit a candle, set it in a dribble of wax on the wobbly table. He spooned succotash from a pot to a plate and set it down carefully on the table.

"We've got no chair," he said. "You could sit on the edge of the bunk."

She came around and sat on the rough log edge of the bunk. The succotash was thin, maybe watered down out of a can, but there was bread to mop it up, a salty hard loaf probably one of them had made. There was coffee, black and bitter. They ate in silence, the two of them standing holding plates in their hands while she sat. The only sound was the scrape of spoons against tin and the breath and snap of the fire in the stovebox. The boys didn't look at each other, only sometimes in a glancing way at her. They chewed carefully. She saw the Adam's apple in the younger boy's neck sliding up and down slowly when he swallowed. Watching him, she began to fill up with vague melancholy.

"I guess those goats must need to be let down," the older one said, low.

She looked toward him. "Yes."

"Well it's been a while but I used to do it. I guess I could help out."

Both of them followed her out into the fine dark rain. They pushed the door back so the candlelight fell outside. In that dim light, silently, Lydia pinned the brown doe, Louise, between her legs and leaned over the goat's back to let down the milk on the ground. It was hard to get her started; a goat was inclined to be cross with any change of her situation. The two boys watched her.

"You don't want to catch that milk?" the older one said finally.

She kept from looking toward them, or toward the two mules browsing the high wet weeds. "I believe the pail and pans are carried at the bottom of the packs," she said. "I don't know if they can easily be got out."

They stood a moment. Then the older one went over and began to pick at the damp pack knots. The other one helped him. They wrestled with the packs and the saddle, rubbed down the mules, wordlessly carried her goods inside the little house. The older boy straddled Rose and held her neck and shoulders between his knees. He looked a little clumsy, and it was a while before he got her to let down into the pail. The younger one stood watching, pushing his forearms down straight into his pockets. He had a look in his face, like a child watching other children playing a game he didn't know.

"My mother used to keep goats," the older boy said. He had lost some of his mutter. In the darkness, in the rain, his voice had a low man's sound, soft-spoken. "She was Quaker. She kept pigs too."

"Where are you from?" she asked him.

"New York."

She looked across the goat's back at him. "I lived near Williamsport, in Pennsylvania. We had neighbors who were Quaker."

He smiled slightly. "Hey," he said. "Have you heard of Six Corners?"

"No."

"Well it's pretty small. But that's where I'm from. It can't be a hundred miles from Williamsport."

She stood and stretched and briefly pressed her hands against the small of her back. "I have a tin of cherries," she said. "They are good with a little fresh milk."

They looked at her. Finally the younger one said, "My mother used to can up cherries."

In the dim, ugly house, the three of them ate cherries and syrup with the hot milk poured over, spooning it up slowly, quietly, off the tin plates. Afterward, she poured a little hot water over flakes of yellow soap in their small chipped basin. They looked at one another but did not deny her. While she did the dishes they made vague motions around the room, until it became clear they were gathering their gear. There was only a little pile of it, once they had put on their coats and chaps — worn plaid blankets stitched together to make a couple of bedrolls, a greasy canvas cook's kit, and another little duffel that held razors, soap, stubs of candle. She gave over the cleaned plates, the wiped-out tin basin, and they stowed them in the dirty cook's sack.

She had seen the place where the horses stood, deep in black mud, puddled brown. It was from guilt that she said, finally, "You might sleep under the shed roof, and go when it is light."

The older boy looked at his feet. Then he looked at her. He was back to muttering again. "We had to ride after dark a lot of times, on outfits we been with. It's nothing. We got oilskins if it keeps raining."

The younger one said, "It's okay, ma'am." His face was serious.

They went out, hauling their saddles with the straps trailing. The air was wet and cold and black. She stood behind them silently while they saddled and tied on their gear. Their boots sucked gently in the mud under the shed roof.

Astride their big horses, in bulky coats and wide-brimmed hats, they seemed less boyish. They looked down at her shyly.

"Good luck to you, ma'am," the younger one said.

"And you."

They turned out across the clearing and went along the little creek into the darkness.

From the ridge, the baited-up meat looked like a spill of red paint. Maybe it was wolves had come up to it: there were a couple of dead animals on the grass there. In the poor light, from a distance, they looked black, bigger than coyote.

Harley rode down slowly off the ridge. He let the horse pick its own way through the scrubby myrtle and tamarack, not hurrying. If it was wolf, it wasn't going anywhere. And he had trained himself away from too much expectation. When he got down where it was stinking, he left the horse standing, reins trailing, while he went to squat beside the kill. They were wolves, both of them. They were already stiff, their coarse coats wet through the guard hairs to the undercoat.

One was male, almost black, and the other a gray female. Mates, he thought, and the female still nursing their litter. He had no good way to find the pups, and who knows how many ears would molder in that unknown den when they starved — the bounty was the same for a pup as a grown wolf and a big litter would've been a nice prize. But he was glad enough for the two he had; he had gone eight or nine days this time without taking a hide at all.

He skinned them with spare and practiced movements, rolled the wet pelts together and tied them from the saddle, stuffed the ears in a little leather bag behind the cantle. The bait was sour, just horns and gnawed carcass making a red place on the grass. He would need to drop a fresh one somewhere, away from this stink. If the den was anywhere close he might still get lucky. The pups ought to be a couple of months old if the season ran to par, and they might yet come out of the ground if they were hungry, might smell a fresh kill and come to it.

He was all afternoon scouting the sidehills, looking for something. There were five or six winter-thin cows and their spindly calves grazing along the bottom of one of the gullies, and for a while he sat looking at them. He went on, finally, but when it started to rain he rode back to where he had seen the cows.

They had gone up the side of the hill under the trees. He sat at the bottom with the knotted reins looped around the horn, pulled his old Wakefield from under the fender of the saddle and touched and counted the load with his fingertips while his eyes stayed in the trees studying the cattle. Then his hands touching the gun went still, and he sat frozen on the horse with the sweet surprise holding him quiet and patient. High against the slope, browsing soundless with the cows, the doe turned haunches to him and grazed slowly uphill.

Harley let himself down carefully from the horse. In the dove-colored rain he moved quietly beneath the trees, setting his feet ball first. All at once he could smell the oily gun and the wet mold of the ground and the bouquet of the dogwood trees, their big cream stars, and it gave him a good, tingling feeling of alertness. The stock of the rifle felt warm and smooth under one hand, the barrel cold and hard and smooth in the other.

The deer turned and came toward him, making no sound. When she saw him, her head lifted with a wisp of grass dangling from the jaw like a beard. He brought the stock of the rifle against his cheek, and then he could smell the strychnine on the skin of his hands. She moved gently, turning, looking at him now with her head canted over one shoulder. Harley squeezed his hand, and as the deer leaped, the butt of the rifle came back hard against his shoulder and the sound popped loud through the silence. The deer, bounding high on springy legs, turned once to touch him with her wide eyes and then was gone into the timber, through the scattering, grunting cattle.

Damn. Damn. Damn. In a moment it had all turned sour again. "Damn!" he said, loud, so it rang in the trees.

The cows were going off down the gully. Irritably, he pointed and shot a calf as it was running bawling after its mother. The cow kept on, her bag swinging heavy between her legs. Squatting on his heels in the rain, he cut the calf up the belly and reached through the hole to knead in the poison, working it in the gut and the muscle with the tips of his fingers. A little rain ran off the brim of his hat and steamed in the puddle of blood around his boots.

By the time he was done, some of the edge had been worn away. He was cold and wet, and the best part of the day had been used up anyway. He wiped his hands on the grass and let the pinto horse take him toward home. There was little enough comfort there. The house crouched dumb and blind on the high bench in the rain. Jack's horse stood droop-necked and dismal inside the strand of rope fence, but there wasn't any smoke coming from the damned stove.

He put his horse in with Jack's and went through the wet weeds to the house. There was a patchy steer hide hung up in the door opening, that was all they had as a door. He pushed it and carried his saddle in. The place was cold. It stank of rot and wet and wolf and maleness. Jack wasn't there. The only light was the daylight that came in gray bars where the chinking had crumbled away between the logs.

Irritably, Harley brought a little wood in and laid a smoky fire in the stove, and while he was fussing with it Jack came up from wherever he had been. He had his rifle in one hand. He used the butt of it to push back the door hide, coming in.

"Where's Danny?" Jack said, as if he thought the two of them ought to be together, though he would have seen there was only Harley's horse standing with his. Harley didn't see a reason to answer him at all. He sat on his blanket on the floor and took out his cards and started to play solitaire.

Jack had a big mustache that maybe hid a harelip, or anyway

a scar on his mouth, and sometimes there would be spittle caught in the whiskers. He must have known it. He had a habit of rubbing his sleeve across his mouth every little while, or rubbing down across the mustache with the edge of his hand. He did it now, using his left hand, though there wasn't any spit on his brush that Harley could see. "Where is he?" Jack said peevishly.

Jack had already set Harley off a little, leaving the stove for him to do, and Harley had a reflex, a quick bitterness, he knew that about himself. He looked at Jack over the cards and felt his face redden all at once. He said, "I'm not his mother, I guess," so it was a gibe. Generally he spoke as little as he could get by with, and looking down at his boots as if he was still a damned kid — he couldn't keep from it. But if he was provoked, or felt on the least wobbly ground that way, he found he could get his look up straight and the words that would come out then would be straight too, and quick. He hadn't ever considered whether it got him anything he wanted.

Jack looked at him and then went back out without a word. Harley kept playing cards. He sat with his back close to the poor heat from the stove. He thought, *I'm not his mother.* He didn't go out after him.

In a while he heard Danny — not his horse on the soft ground crossing the bench, but the sound Danny made wheezing, as he lifted his saddle off and carried it across to the shack. He had bad lungs. He said a cow had poked a horn through one of them once, and he always had wheezed after that. He came in with his saddle and set it down and looked at Harley. Then he opened the stove and shook the wood around.

"It's cold in here," he said.

Harley didn't look up. "Jack was here first," he said, low. "He never got the stove going."

Danny said, "Where is he?"

"I guess he's looking for you." He snorted. He turned over his cards steadily by threes.

Danny went and stood in the door, holding the hide back and

looking out for Jack. Once, Harley looked out too, without getting up from his cards. He could see past Danny, Jack coming down from the scrub trees above the bench, jumping off the high rocks and carrying his rifle down toward the house. Danny stood in the door waiting for him.

"What's going on."

Jack shrugged. "I ran into one of those friends of yours," he said. His mouth spread out under the edge of his mustache but it wasn't a smile. He shrugged again and went by Danny, bending his head down to go in under his arm. Danny followed him. Harley, sitting over his cards, looked at both of them without saying anything.

Jack got out his pocketknife and sat in the corner in the gray darkness and started to pare his fingernails. Danny just stood and waited, looking at him, wheezing faintly. Finally Jack said, "He seen me put down one of his steers." He was looking at the tips of his fingers, examining them carefully in the dim light and then trimming the nails one by one with the edge of his knife. "I think I lost him. Anyway he didn't follow me back. I've been sitting up there a while watching for him."

Danny was always careful about touching his face with his hands—he was scared of the strychnine. He crooked up one shoulder now and bent his face to the scratchy sleeve of his coat, as if his eyes were itching. "Which one of them was it?" he said, in a cranky way.

"The Indian."

"How good a look did he get?"

Jack tipped his head to one side, raised his brows. He said nothing, just that indifferent shrug.

Danny said, "They'll be along, you know. Tonight or tomorrow. They'll come along here looking for you."

Jack folded his knife and pushed it down in a front pocket of his pants. Then he spread his fingers out on his knees and admired them. He didn't say anything.

"I don't want trouble with them," Danny said finally. He had used to work with those two, the Indian and Whiteaker. He liked to worry a lot, out loud, about baiting up cows of theirs. But he and Jack had been together a long time — since before the cow business went to hell, before Harley had thrown in with them. And it was a long time ago he'd worked with those other two up on the Spokane River.

Jack looked at him. "You done your share of cow killing," he said. "Just like the rest of us."

There was a silence. Then Danny said it again. "I don't want trouble." He hadn't much of a temper but he was stubborn, he just didn't give ground. For a while Harley had thought Jack was the hard one. But he knew better by now. Jack had more piss, that was all. Danny waited and after a while he said, "They've been pretty much looking the other way so far. But they won't let us rub their noses in it. I know the both of them that well. And the other one, Whiteaker, he tracks pretty good. He'll follow you right on back here, don't fool yourself on that. If Blue didn't get a good look at you, it won't matter once they see what hole you run into."

Jack didn't look at Danny. He was studying his hands, and he sat as if he was absorbed in that, indifferent. Danny just waited for him. You could hear Danny's little wheeze, as if he had run out of breath. Harley watched both of them without quite looking up from his cards. He thought of saying something. He felt, if it came down to it, the three of them were an outfit, and they ought to stand like one. *We ought not to do any backing up,* he thought of saying. But he couldn't get it to come out. He turned the cards over slowly, silently.

After a while Jack said, "A man's got to make a living, Danny." There wasn't any sharp edge on it. He said it straight, like he thought it cleared up something, and his look at Danny was straight too, not smirking, just grave and thoughtful.

Harley looked at Danny too. Danny never did make any sort of answer to what Jack had said. Only finally, tiredly, he rubbed his itchy eyes with the knuckles of his strychnine-smelly hands.

From the hill, stopping at the fence line to let down the rails, Tim thought the house looked small and squat and dark. But it stood in a good place, with its back against the steep ridge and the front looking out on the spring, puddled up in a shallow half-moon pond, and then the long upslope of grass. They had cleared out some trees on the north side of the house too and put a shed there, and the grass had spread to fill the ground between the stumps. All the grass stood green this time of year, long and heavy-headed with narrow tracks beaten through it where the cattle walked.

There were a couple of dozen cows and their calves inside the fence, maybe two-thirds of the spring count they were hoping for after a cold winter and wolfers taking cows now and then when no better bait offered itself up. Their two sections might support seventy or eighty head over the winter, not more than that. If they wanted to do better, they'd have to give in and go to cutting hay, like Oberfield did, doling it out on the snow. They had been digging in their heels on that. Neither of them had ever run a mower or stacked hay, they had learned cowboying before the range was in fence. Hell, they had quit a job once, when the boss put them to digging a well.

Blue was there next to the shed, sliding the saddle off his long-legged roan, dragging it over under the slanted roof. He was half deaf in one ear but he could hear a cow's low bellow from a long way off and he turned and stood watching up the hill while Tim and the dog brought the three cows and the calves through. Tim, riding down slowly toward him, saw him shrugging his shoulders as if his collarbone was hurting him again.

"He's lame," Blue said, leaning his head at the bay horse. The horse's shank was swollen a little; he set his hoof down delicately, not quite limping.

"You and him both," Tim said. There was a scabbed-over scrape on Blue's forehead under the shadow of the hat.

Blue pulled his shoulders up gently. "I tried, but nothing broke," he said, letting out his slow smile.

"How about the horse," Tim said. By now he had seen the mud in a yellowy dry smear where the roan had come down on his off side.

"Mine? He's okay. Yours is lame."

"You said that." Tim slid the saddle off and swung it up on the rack in the shed. He pulled out the bit, stood wiping the bay's wet coat with a scrap of sacking while Blue watched him, smoking a cigarette. Then he led the horse out through the stumps to the edge of the pond. Their coming and going had hardened several little trails in the bank, slickened now and muddy. He stood with the horse out in the pond and kneaded the shank gently in the cold brown water.

"The Buck's trail give way. He cut his shank," he said. After a while, when Blue didn't say anything, he said, "That trail tears like paper in this kind of weather."

Blue shrugged. "Long way around, otherwise."

"Long way down," Tim said, low.

Blue stood behind him and smoked his cigarette, letting the smoke out slowly. "We need to go up to Loeb's old shack and see if Turnbow is still squatting there," he said after a silence.

Tim looked toward him.

"I jumped a cow shooter," Blue said. "I didn't see him good, but he had a buckskin horse. One of those wolfers with Danny had a buckskin, as I remember."

Tim went back to working the bay's shank. The leg was a little puffy along the scabby line of the cut. *Well hell.*

"One of us was bound to catch them at it, sooner or later," he said in a low voice. "Now we can't let it pass anymore. They ought to know that."

After a while Blue said, "They know it."

Tim walked the horse out of the water. Blue's roan was rolling in the grass, looking long-legged and big-barreled, clumsy, rubbing off the caked mud. Tim stood in the dusk in the fine rain, watching him. He held the bay by the cheek strap of the halter. *Danny won't want trouble with us. Maybe they've got smart, packed up and moved.* He didn't say it. It had been six or seven years since he and Blue had worked with Danny Turnbow up on the Spokane River, and when they'd seen him camping at Loeb's abandoned shack he'd been sporting a rifle, and a testiness that was new since those days on the Spokane.

He let the bay loose, watched him walk away across the darkening grass. The horse wasn't limping quite, but he stepped like a tired old man, or a kid used to barefoot, wearing tight new shoes. Tim's own knee ached, his feet were wet and cold. Watching the bay made him think of it.

"Have we got carbolic anywhere?"

Blue looked at him. "No. What for?"

He ducked his head. "I heard it was good for cuts."

Blue shrugged, watching him. Then he put out the cigarette under the heel of his boot and went into the dark at the back of the shed where the wood was stacked up in leaning ricks. Tim went through the damp gray dusk to the house. The stove was dead cold. He laid a fire from the scraps of wood left in the box. There was veal off a dogie calf hanging up in the cool room, and he cut off bits close to the bone and put them in with the pot of beans that had cooked and then gone cold on the back of the stove. Blue brought in the new wood, holding it one-armed, saving his sore collarbone.

"There's a woman has taken up Angell's claim on the Jump-Off Creek," Tim said without turning around.

Blue let the wood down. "You see her?"

He nodded.

In a moment Blue said, "That place is well gone to seed."

Tim didn't say anything. Then finally he did. "I guess she knows it."

# ❖ 7 ❖

*8 April* Lost the way on poor directions but I am here now and glad for it, tho it is bad as I knew it would be, the stove rusted clear through, the roof rotted, the logs poor fitted and mildewed, the yard where the Animals must stand all Mud and stones. I have not lost Heart, having done so in years past and no false hopes this time. There are Graces at all events, the site well chosen with the good cold Stream in front and must be trout in it when the snow is done melting and the water clears. The trees are cut down all around. There is a Window, small & unglassed, but I believe it stands to let in the low Winter Sun from the South. I am greatly sore & tired, having come all day across these dark Mountains in unending rain, but the black Mule has proved a good choice, he is steady as the old Mule, Lester, I rode on the ice when I was 12. There were old dark stains on the ticking of the Bed and Mice or others had been into the fill so I burned the bedsack and must sleep on the bare wood of the Bunk if not in Mud, suppose I ought to be glad for tiredness, I can sleep Anywhere if tired enough. Every thing I own save the poor Beasts is in a heap here in the center of this room and if I mean to keep it whole I must before I sleep cover all against the leaking, rake old tins & leavings outside the door, burn a camphor stick against vermin, set my few mouse traps along the walls. And hope for better Weather & Strength in the days coming. I have put out in the night the 2 boys I found here, they had taken up living in the empty house. Those were Troubles I could not borrow, as I am scarce likely to make my own living in this poor place and coming West I have seen idle men Everywhere about in La Grande and Boise and Missoula and in the Papers woeful news of the falling price of Wheat & Cattle both. They were polite & forebearing, for which reason I am sorry.

In the morning they went back up toward the Bear's Camp Mountain and picked up the trail of the cow shooter on the buckskin horse. He had gone quickly at first, leaving a broad track of broken stems and slurred prints in mud. But within the first half mile or so he'd seen there was nobody behind him and after that the trail came down to dim hoof marks abraded by rain, and infrequent sign in the wet brush. They scouted the faded trail slowly for the better part of five miles, until it was lost altogether, under somebody else's sloppy track. Tim walked over the ground carefully, sorting it out, while Blue stood leaning on the rump of his horse, smoking one of his thin brown cigarettes. Three or four horses had slid down the little hill from the southeast and muddied up the ravine and then gone off to the north in a straggling line.

"Loeb's old place is just up there," Tim said. "This guy made a beeline for the shack and then all of them came back a ways along his trail to spoil his sign."

Blue looked up the hill. Finally he let smoke out, looking sideward at Tim. "They could've packed up and gone."

Tim didn't look toward him. "Maybe."

They rode silently up to Loeb's. There wasn't any rain to speak of, just the trees dribbling whenever the wind came up. It was cold, though, and they both rode in a hunched way, with their necks pulled down as far as they could get them inside the collars of their coats.

Old Loeb had been a hermit, had chosen his site for its high aerie feel, the little treeless bench with the mountain shooting up steep behind it and dropping off in long timbered fells in front. The sky hung in shaggy ribbons there, low in the trees, wet. They could see the place through the drizzling gray from quite a ways downslope, could see it sitting high on that bench staring blind across the tips of the trees, with the dirtier grizzle of smoke seeping into the overcast and the horses standing tail-to-head inside a strand of rope.

Blue shook his head and let the roan stop, as soon as they got where they could see one of the horses was a buckskin. "Hell."

Tim waited for him. They sat looking up the slope. In a while Blue made a cigarette, tapping his forefinger carefully against the little sack of tobacco. But he didn't light it. He ran it back and forth between a thumb and a finger.

"You'll know this guy if you see him?" Tim said.

"Big curly coat was about all I saw. And the horse."

They sat in silence. Then Blue said, "We could let it go. It wasn't one of our steers anyhow. Was a Box O. I guess Oberfield can take the loss well enough." Looking up the hill, he put the unlit cigarette inside his coat, in his shirt pocket.

In a while Tim said stubbornly, "It might not be this guy. We ought to see whether it is or not."

Blue made a sour sound.

They held their carbines across the pommels of the saddles and put the horses sway-butting up the slope. The dogs went ahead, their nostrils smoking and coats standing out full in the chill. When they broke across the front edge of the bench, they could smell ill-cured or green hides, and rankness of wolf. Tim had left the bay behind to heal his leg. The gray mare he rode was fidgety, timid. She tossed her muzzle against the stink, and started to walk sideways. He had a hard time keeping her turned, with one hand occupied, holding on to the Miller rifle.

Danny Turnbow came out of the shack and stood just under the overhanging eave, watching them come. He had a big notch in his chin, a thick straight forelock of hazel hair. When they stopped the horses a dozen yards out, he pushed back at his hair with a self-conscious gesture of his right hand. "Blue," he said. "Tim. Long time no see."

Tim said, straight, "We thought maybe you would've moved someplace else by now."

Turnbow smiled slowly, looking at them from under his eyebrows, chin down. "This place sits good and high, varmints like it high. Game's good too. For the baits." He kept smiling gently. When they'd known him in the Spokane country he'd had a soft and wise hand with nervous horses. He was known for it.

Tim felt something, maybe it was embarrassment. "We've seen a few baits around," he said. "They've been cows, sometimes."

Turnbow shook his head, looked beyond them down the long timbered slope. "I seen some of that too," he said. He was solemn. "They ought to use leg-holds if they can't get an honest bait."

Tim said, "Wolf is smart. Hard to get into a trap."

Turnbow shrugged without answering. He was still smiling slightly.

There was a silence. "I guess the fur season is about done," Tim said.

Danny made a loose gesture. "State is still paying five dollars each. Don't need a hide at all for that, and they don't give a damn how those ears look." He grinned, persuading them. "By fall, won't be a timber wolf alive from Meacham to Summerville."

Blue hadn't said anything up to now, but he wouldn't let that one go by. He said, low-voiced, "We lost more cows to shooting, lately, than anything else."

There was a stiff little silence. Then Danny lifted his brow in solemn surprise. " 'S'at so?" He pushed back his hair.

"The truth is, we've been tracking a cow shooter," Tim said. "Probably he's a wolfer. We wondered if you knew him."

Danny shook his head. He still looked solemn, unsmiling. "We haven't seen anybody in quite a while. We're pretty much out of the way up here."

The gray horse hadn't quit squirming. Tim wished he had both hands to head her. He said, holding the mare hard, "He would be riding a buckskin horse like that short-legged one you've got over there. He'd be wearing a curly Montana-style coat."

Turnbow, holding his chin down, looking at them low like that, said, "A lot of men wear Montana coats. A lot of men have got buckskin horses." His voice was easy, faintly sorrowful.

Tim kept on stubbornly. "We were tracking him over behind Bear's Camp," he said. "Your tracks went through there too, so we thought maybe you saw him. It was your horses going through there that spoiled his sign for us."

Danny seemed to think about what he ought to say. He hunted for something in the middle distance. Then a boot moved below the scabby hide hung in the door opening of the shack. Tim got a quick heat in his chest. He put his thumb on the hammer of his carbine. Maybe Blue eared his all the way back, because he heard a faint clatching sound and Danny's face jerked as if somebody had goosed him. "Don't jump the gun now," he said, but it wasn't clear who he meant it for.

A hand pushed the hide and then a boy came out to stand under the eave of the roof. They'd seen him once before with Turnbow, a kid named Harley Osgood. He was thin and tall, his pimply face set high above a very long neck, and above that a flat-brimmed hat as wide as a boarding house platter. Under the hat he showed sorrel red hair in a long shag, and skin that looked dead white around the pimples. He stood next to Danny, looking down at his boots. He had no curly coat, just a thin canvas jacket with stains on the cuffs and across the front. Danny didn't say anything to him. He shifted his weight making room for him in a slight way, and gave Tim and Blue a look, maybe of embarrassment. The kid, Osgood, had a big-handled pistol sitting up high in a holster at his waist.

The Adam's apple in the boy's long neck skated up and down once slowly. Then he looked over at Tim. Maybe he had been getting up his gumption. "I figured an Indian could track a mouse over a flat rock," he said. His voice was low and hoarse, and his face grew suddenly blotchy and red. "What's wrong with yours there? He lose his eye for it when he cut off his braids?"

Blue had a pretty high boiling point. He made a short sound like a laugh, without saying anything. But there was a stiffness in the air. Even the dogs were standing up, with the hair lifted along their shoulders. Osgood kept looking at Tim in a sullen, wild way.

Danny said slowly, "Why don't you all come on in and set." He touched the edge of the doorhide. "We got a pot heating up."

Blue began to smile. "I'll bet you do," he said, low, and Turnbow made a smile of his own, sliding his eyes sideways to Osgood.

"Yeah, well." He scratched the back of his neck with raggy black fingernails. "The truth is, the coffee's pretty damn bitter. We been using them grounds since last week," He eyed them again, from under his brows. "Times are hard. You know what I mean?"

There was a waiting silence. Tim couldn't tell what Blue might be wanting to do by now. "I thought there were three or four of you living here, last time we came by," he said.

Turnbow swung his hand vaguely, looking past Tim. "There's three of us, that's right. Jack's in bed. Got ahold of a little strychnine maybe, off his hands. He's sick as death. Been in bed four days now."

In a while Blue said, "Maybe it was the coffee made him sick." Turnbow smiled slightly. "Might be it was."

Tim shifted his seat carefully, looking sidelong at Blue. Blue shrugged up both his shoulders, maybe not just easing the ache of his collarbone.

"I guess not," Blue said. Maybe he was answering Turnbow's offer to come in and have a cup.

Tim said, in a moment, "You keep an eye out for a guy in a curly coat, riding a buckskin horse." He wanted to say something more, something about hanging him, but it sounded stupid or cocky, any way he could think of saying it.

He thought the kid might make some kind of a sour answer, but he didn't, he just stood next to Danny, looking down at the toes of his boots. You would think you could kick him around like a stone, he had that aspect now. But he had stood before, all dare and hot piss, giving them a straight look.

"Sure," Danny said, nodding, solemn. "We'll watch."

In the silence afterward, Tim heard Blue shifting his weight on the saddle and then turning the roan. Tim didn't want to turn his back on Osgood, or on the other, the Montana man, inside the shack, but he did, finally, giving Danny a look as he swung around. He jigged the mare when he saw Blue was doing the same, and they went pretty fast across the bench with the dogs running to keep up. When they got to the tree line they slowed down, and after a while let the horses walk. Blue took the made cigarette out of his inside pocket and smoked it.

Tim remembered suddenly a sorrel horse Blue had owned once, that would buck like the devil every time he lit up a cigarette. It had been a good horse otherwise, but Blue never had been able to break him of that little peculiarity, and he'd wound up trading him for a big, strong-looking bay that proved later to have tender feet. Tim didn't know why he thought of that now.

"I guess there wasn't any point in pushing it," Blue said, not looking at him.

Tim pulled his shoulders up. Finally he said, "I guess we can wait and see what they do." He could hear his heart beating inside his ears.

Where the chinking had fallen out, the gaps between the logs began finally to show grayness. Lydia stood stiffly and went out in the muddy clothes she'd not taken off the day before. There was no rain, just the damp chill raising the flesh of her arms, and the clouds caught in the tops of the trees along the edges of the clearing.

The back of the house stood up close against the high slope of a ridge. There were trees still standing there, where maybe Angell hadn't wanted to log on the steep grade. She went up under the trees and squatted and then came down to the creek and washed in that cold water without soap or towel, no telling where those were in the heap of goods in the shack. She shook out her cold wet hands, blinked wet eyelashes. She made the best of the unstill water as a looking glass and with stiff fingers worked through the tangle of her hair, retrieving and rearranging the few hairpins she could find, shaping a small, unruly knot. She would have been satisfied with simple tidiness, but in a while gave up ever reaching it and went back through the brush fence to the animals.

In the bare daylight, in the mud, she let down the goats, catching up a little in a chipped white coffee cup and drinking it down while standing there beside the goats, with her fingers lapped around the cup and her face held close over the little warmth of it.

Across the rim of the cup she looked at Angell's place. Another ridge rose up along the south, steep and high as the one behind the house. The Jump-Off Creek ran between them, along the flattish bottomland where Angell had cut his crossties. It was a narrow clearing, a hundred yards wide at most, running up and down the banks of the creek, maybe twenty acres altogether of weeds and grass and thin saplings and brush growing among the stumps. Where the brush pen was, and in front of the house, nothing grew, it was all mud and rocks and deep tracks of men's boots, horses' shod feet. There were slick muddy trails at the near edge of the creek, too, where they'd come for the water.

Lydia stood and stared at all of it for quite a while. She had spent some of the night sleepless on the bare bunk, folded up in her mother's Windmill quilt, fitting her bony hip and shoulder into a gap where two logs joined. And in the darkness, lying a long time awake, listening to the dripping roof and the rats chewing the garbage in the yard, she had begun finally, stubbornly, to tally the work. It was an old solace. Her mother hadn't ever liked to have her list them like that, all the things needing doing ranked from worst to least, first to last. *You'll make the heart go right out of you.* But Lydia always had liked to see the whole shape to her work. When there was time for it, and paper, she would write the jobs down and afterward mark a line through every one as it was finished. In the blackness last night, inside the cold stinking house, she'd made the list against her closed eyes, inside her head, going over it slowly and over it, getting the order right. Now in the gray daylight, standing looking at the mud and the high wet weeds, looking at the whole shape, all the things needing doing, she felt her heart tighten up like a fist.

She cut brush all day, grubbing out thickets by the roots with a blunt mattock, leaving the tall skinny saplings and the bracken ferns for the goats. The weather stayed damp and cold, the sky coming down low so there was no seeing how high the ridges stood. But the rain held off and she got warm enough, working. For a while she wore Lars's big gray coat but as soon as she'd worked up a sweat it came off and she was able to get by with just the green sweater buttoned all the way up over the navy waist she'd worn for traveling.

Every little while she stood and filed an edge onto the mattock and then piled up the brush on a tarp and dragged it behind her across the rough ground to the house. She laid out the new fence starting at the back corner of the house and going up under the trees on the steep slope where the ground was not worn slick, tramped to mud. The hill was duffy with moss and old brown needles, and the trees would maybe keep off the rain.

When the brush was laid in place, she dug a ditch along it for the dead-hedge, using the mattock and a spade, and pushing down the soil around the roots with the mattock and the heel of her boot. The ground was rocky on the hillside, under the shallow duff, and it was matted with root. The ditch was slow going. Often she stood up straight, pushing the ache out of her back and then plucking at the front of the sweater and the blue cotton waist, letting cold air in deliberately under her breasts, where she sweated. She had Lars's big gloves. Her hands slid inside them so a blister was gradually rubbed on one hand, along the web at the base of the thumb. She wound a clean rag around that hand, inside the glove. She scraped the mattock along the ground stubbornly, huffing white breath on the still, cold air.

At dusk, in a frosty cold, she drove the mules and the goats inside the stiff new fence and let the goats down and again drank a cupful, standing there. She remembered suddenly, tasting the sweet heat of the milk: she had not made a meal. And remembering it, her stomach clenched with hunger.

It was black and cold inside the shack. She made a fire in the stove, coaxing it slow and smoking from the wet wood. She fried a patty of corn meal and bolted it down, standing over the stove.

She drank hot water, having no patience, this late, to get at the coffee among her piled-up stores. Afterward she took the dead rats out of the traps and set the springs on them again and heated salt and soda water in a pail. In the high jumping shadow of candlelight, she pushed a stiff boar's hair brush steadily back and forth along the peeling, mildewed walls, the bedframe, the teetery three-legged table, and then made up her bed for the second night, on the clean bare logs of the bunk. She shook the bedding out and went along the quilts cautiously, holding up a candle, looking for vermin.

Sitting on the edge of the bed in the poor light, she wrote tiredly, crosswise over the printed vertical columns of the accounting ledger she had taken over for a journal.

*9 April* Cut brush all day to make a Fence. I have not worked this hard in a while so I am tired but now I have a place for the beasts to stand out of mud anyway. If I'm to wear clean stockings in the morning must do up a little wash yet tonight. O I would trade all for a hot bath but too tired to lift the water myself. Believe I was up 3 times or 4 in the night to take dead Rats from traps and reset. Have killed 16 Rats so far. The rain has quit but it is still cold & the sky low.

She sat on the edge of the bunk a while with the book closed in one hand, her eyes closed too. Then she undid her boots, lay down stiffly in stiff dirty stockings. The quilt had gone dank, clammy, all day in the leaky house, but there was still a little clean mothball smell in it. She pulled the edge up to her eyes.

## ✿ 10 ✿

Harley Osgood hated the leg-hold traps. He left them jangling on his saddle most of the day, until it was plain he wouldn't have any luck with finding game. Then, to keep from Danny's righteous yelling, he got down off his horse and set a couple of the damned things. He chained one to a tree, pried open the jaws and balanced a piece of meat gingerly on the trigger, then kicked a little duff over the jaws and the chain. He didn't worry about his smell being on the iron because they wouldn't catch any wolves in the things anyway; he knew better than that. And the truth was, he was afraid to touch a trap that was set. He had a stupid fear of the things, from breaking two fingers in a squirrel trap when he was a little kid, and a healthy fear, from seeing what a wolf's leg looked like, caught in the sprung jaws.

It started to rain as he was setting the last one. It was half dark by then, so after thinking about it, he rode down the Jump-Off Creek to that old shack. He was quite a bit closer to it than to the place on the high bench, and the last time he had gone by the Jump-Off shack there had been a couple of cowboys living there, they had been young as him. He figured he would get in under the roof with them and get dry, wait out the wet and the dark. Maybe they'd play cards. He had lately learned how to play euchre, he was anxious to play it whenever he could. It wasn't like he had anything waiting for him up on the bench. Jack would have played cards with him, but he never could win when he played euchre with Jack.

He stuck his cold left hand inside his coat, between the snaps in the front, but that didn't help the right hand holding the reins or his ears hanging out cold below the hat. Every little while rain ran off the front of his hat brim, dribbling on his wrists and the sleeve of his coat where he reached out holding the horse to a straight path. "Shit," he said, in a flat way, every time it happened. He had a habit of swearing when he was alone, for the little bit of cold comfort in it.

It wasn't all the way dark yet when he came out of the trees into the long clearing. All the light left in the day seemed to lay in that open place. He could see from where he was, a woman walking down from the trees behind the house. She must have seen him too. She stood and looked a minute and then went on quicker and stood waiting in front, beside the door, with her arms folded up on the front of a big old coat.

He hadn't thought about those cowboys maybe moving on, and somebody else squatting in the house. Shit! He sat his horse under the skimpy cover at the edge of the trees and looked across at the woman, the rain falling straight down in the open clearing between them. But then he went ahead. He was hungry, and teeth-chattering cold, and hell, they were just squatters.

When he came up in the yard, something started a sudden scared racket behind the house. He heard the brush fence cracking and when the woman heard it she made a desperate face and went around there quickly, flapping her muddy big skirt. But the goats had got out by then, two of them scooting off through the stumps, up the long clearing, bleating a silly alarm. The woman made a tired, helpless gesture, lifting one hand, as she stood there watching them run away. Harley sat up straighter, without smiling. He had got to like it a little, the way people and livestock pulled up short and their eyes rolled white when they smelled the wolf on him.

He stopped his horse and waited. She was tall as a man, lean, and as old as Danny Turnbow. There were muddy fingerprints on the brim of her old man's hat, as if she had taken it off or set it on with dirty hands. She stood stiffly along the hole the goats had made in the dead-hedge and looked back at him. He dropped his own look down to his cold hand clasping the reins.

"Ma'am," he said, without looking at her. He didn't say anything about the goats. "The squatters' rights been already taken up here," he said in a low voice. "Me and two others have been living here all winter." He had thought out how much of a lie to tell, and he delivered it as briefly as might be. "I don't mind sharing the roof with your family tonight, though, since it's raining."

The woman's face set slowly, not quite as if he had provoked her, but as if she was getting hold of a stubbornness. She pushed her hands down in the pockets of her big coat. "I have bought the deed outright from Mr. Angell," she said in a level voice, cold as clay. He could tell it was the truth just by the way she stood there, and a little heat began to come up in his neck. He felt stupid, all at once.

Without his deciding to do it, he sat up higher in the saddle and looked at the woman recklessly. "You don't say," he said, letting the words out short so he knew they sounded disbelieving. He didn't know what he expected out of that. It had come out without thinking, on his sudden, unexpected temper.

She lifted her big chin slightly and drew her mouth up in small pleats. The look she gave him was pink, straight, bristly. "I'm sorry for it, but I must turn you away, as there isn't room under the roof," she said, without sounding sorry at all, only sharp and very well decided.

He felt his own face going red and he tried to stop it from doing that. But for a while he could only sit there feeling that bright thing like embarrassment, and himself holding straight in the saddle. He wished wildly that he had come to her in the first place with his hat in his hand, she would maybe then have let him sleep on a shakedown bed next to the stove. But there was no going back to that now.

She said, with her mouth still drawn up and stiff, "If you are hungry I can spare milk for you." She was watching him. The rain felt cold as snow. Her look made him suddenly sorry for himself, and piteous.

He pulled up his shoulders gloomily and looked down at his cold hands. "No," he said, in a low, miserable way. "I'm not on the grub line yet." Without any warning, his eyes sprang with tears. In desperate embarrassment he jerked his horse around and kicked it, kept kicking it until they had run into the dark under the trees. He was crying by then, stupidly, helplessly. *Shit*, he thought. *Shit!* He wiped his face on the sleeve of his cold, muddy coat.

"Horsefaced old bitch," he said running the words together loud and wet. "Stupid old woman." It was a long-standing comfort. He had used to go out in the corn or down along the rock road below the house when he was twelve years old, fourteen, and swear out loud at his mother. *Old bitch cunt slut.* Swearing until he had quit crying. The last occasion for it, he had backed one of his sisters up against the barn wall in the shadows under the hay rick and squeezed the small buds of her breasts in both his hands. He remembered suddenly, the look that had come into her face. Her eyes had gone so wide-open that the whites had showed all the way around. He was too old to be whipped by that time, but his mother's husband had whipped him for it anyway, and afterward he had gone down the road, swearing out loud, and never had gone back. Thinking of that old humbling, now, a heat began to crawl in his face, making the pimply skin itch. "You damn whore!" he shouted out, and got a cold solace from the echo of it in the black trees.

# ❀ 11 ❀

A south wind came up from the Grande Ronde overnight and pushed the clouds up billowy and white. The sky broke clean and pale blue behind them. In the sunlight, the air was watery, dazzling. Lydia did a quick washing and laid the clothes, the milk rags, the towels out on the brush fence where they steamed faintly and shivered against the hedge whenever the wind gusted. The water after the washing was fawn-colored, tepid, but she wrung a clean rag in it and did a meager washup herself, standing on the little braid-rug barefoot in her shift. The washrag felt cold, sandy. She took long fast swipes, only delaying at her feet, poking scrupulously at the black filth between her toes.

Afterward, she took the bucksaw and the mattock and froe and went up the Jump-Off Creek, under the trees, where she was about done bucking and making shingles off a windfallen cedar. She changed off, sawing through a butt and then splitting it, piling the shingles on a tarp and dragging the hillock behind her back to the house before she bucked the next one. The sawing was tedious, trying. There was a tooth out near the draw end of the saw and when she pulled it back too far, it hung up. But she drove the froe neatly enough, with the blunt end of the mattock, a few blows down through the butt of the log, the shingles peeling off in clean reddish slabs, arm-long, thick as her wrist. It was cold in the shade. She kept the coat buttoned up. Her breath shot out white in a noisy burst whenever the saw hung up.

The roof was low but she could not clamber up on it ladderless, hauling the long shakes and the nails, the hammer. When she had brought the splitting to an end, she sawed down a thin yellow pine tree and trimmed it and made out of it a homely ladder with four rungs. It was heavy, wide-legged. She horsed it up against the eave of the house and climbed up on it with the shakes pinched under an arm two or three at a time. She piled the shakes up slowly in long, neat ranks below the crown, going down the ladder and up repeatedly. She had to pull her big skirt around out of the way, gather some of it up in the belt, as it kept hanging on the broken shakes and on the nubbin ends of the ladder.

The nails went up with her last, in the pockets of Lars's coat, and she laid the shakes from the eave edges, nailing them down on the old rotten roof. The roof was grown over with club moss, the nails went in softly, without getting a hold. She would need to cut long poles afterward and tie them down at either end, across the shakes.

When she had about finished one pitch up to the crown, she heard a calf bawl faintly and saw Mr. Whiteaker and his dog coming across the long clearing from the North Fork of the Meacham. There was a skinny piebald calf straddled wet across the neck of his horse, on the front of his saddle. It was crying thinly and steadily as he came.

She climbed down from the roof, with the front of the coat swinging heavily, full of nails. She pulled the dress loose from the belt and smoothed it, standing in front of the house waiting as he came up in the yard.

"The mother was a CrossTie," he said, without quite looking at her. "So this here is yours."

She stepped up to him and reached to take the slimy calf, staggering a moment beneath the weight and then stiffening to tote it inside the house. She laid it down on the mud and got a clean rag and began to towel off the sticky wet membranes. The man came and stood in the doorway behind her.

"Is the cow dead then?" she said, looking around at him.

"Yes, ma'am. I figured if you had a sugar tit you could maybe nurse him along. We do that if we've got the time. Or I didn't know but what one of your goats might let him suckle."

She nodded without saying anything. Then she said, looking at him again, "Do you know what it was that killed the cow, Mr. Whiteaker?" She had in mind the carcass of that poor cow, baited with poison, but he said, "I guess maybe the calf was born crosswise. It was already born when I came on it. The cow was down and she died on me before I could get her up." He was standing in the doorway, turning his hat in both hands, not leaning against the jamb. His head and shoulders looked hunched under the low ceiling. With the light behind him she couldn't see his face, it was a featureless shadow.

She nodded again. She looked away from him, around to the calf, but she felt the man standing in the door, not making a move to go.

"You've got a lot done," he said after a while. He might have meant the stiff new fence, the roof, the cleared brush. But he was standing inside the door of the house, where there was little enough done, most all of her goods still not put away, standing in one pile under the damp tarp. The quilts had been pulled up smooth on the bare frame of the bed, but there were the traps set out under the bed and behind the stove, and a big rat dead in one, along the wall next to the door. So she made a little indifferent sound, without looking toward him. She kept at the calf, wiping the mucus out of its eyes, ears, lifting it by the tail to stand knob-kneed and unsteady. Behind her the man's shadow moved, she felt the light come in across her back. She stood, gathering up her damp, splintery skirts, and went out after him. She put her hand up flat above her eyes to shade against the thin, bright sunlight.

"Was it you who left the pie?" she asked him, before he had quite put his boot to the stirrup.

He turned and looked at her, ducking his chin. "Yes."

She had stood under the trees the day before and watched him come up to her house, carrying the parcel wrapped in newspaper and a towel, balanced across the pommel of the saddle. Down the long, cleared valley, when he had hallooed the house, the sound had seemed a faint wordless piping. He had come slowly on afterward and sat a moment on the horse looking at the crooked line of the new brush fence going up the hill behind the house. Then he had gone around past the shut-up window to the door and put his parcel down on a stump, not getting off the horse to do it, just leaning over from the saddle and leaving the towel folded around it so it sat on the stump in a lumpish bundle. She did not know why she had stayed there at the high end of the creek, in the cold damp shadow beneath the trees, not going down to speak to him, just standing holding the bucksaw down in her hands and watching him silently.

"Wait," she said, murmuring. "I'll bring you the tin." She went in and found it and brought it out to him with his piece of clean towel folded up inside it. He put his hat on his head, settling it carefully, and took the plate from her with both hands.

"It was a very good pie," she said, and smiled a little. "I am not able to make a decent one myself, I have a heavy hand with the rolling pin."

He ducked his chin again. He turned the plate in his hands. Then he said, looking just past her, "When I was a kid I worked as a cook's monkey over in Idaho. The cook was named Sweet. He took the time to teach me the trade. He said he'd seen years when a good cowboy couldn't buy himself a job, but a good cook could pretty much always find work. He was right about that. I guess I spent as many summers cooking as I ever did cowboying. It's stood me and Blue through a few lean times."

She nodded, surprised. Her notion of him felt somewhat undone. "You are lucky, there, Mr. Whiteaker."

He shifted his weight as if he might leave, but then he stood where he was. "We've got nine cows of yours," he said suddenly. "If you've got Angell's branding iron from him, or one of your own, we'd get your calves done along with ours. We'll be starting up pretty soon."

She had watched the branding of a single heifer calf as she had stood on the railroad platform beside the stockyards in North Platte, Nebraska. That was her experience of it. It was not clear, from what Mr. Whiteaker had said, if he meant to do it for her, or show her how it was done.

"I have got the CrossTie brand from the real estate man," she said. "I guess it would be good to keep the same."

"Yes."

She nodded and looked at him stoutly. "For fairness sake and for my own instruction, I expect you will let me lend a hand. I am quick to learn, and somewhat stronger than I appear."

He dropped his head, hunting for something in the mud. "We have worked a few branding crews with a woman holding down an end," he said slowly. "On a small outfit it's usual for the man's wife to pitch in, or his daughters if he has them."

She nodded a second time. "I am used to doing that myself," she said, smiling slightly.

He pinched the pie tin in his fingers, turning it. Then he put it inside his kit bag. While he was fiddling with the tie-downs she said, without asking a question of him, "I have not ridden out at all, to get in my calves."

He looked at her sidelong. After a while he said, "Claud didn't get around to a count, or a branding either, last year, and he would've lost a few to weather since then. We've been over this ground pretty well ourselves. These nine calves might be all there is out of CrossTie cows."

She had half expected it. She tightened up her mouth but in a moment let it out, smiling grimly. "I suppose I had better grow squashes then, if I'm not to starve."

Mr. Whiteaker gave her a cautious look. "You know where the Walker Ranch is?"

"No."

"Mike Walker has got a place down near the Oberfield Road, a wife and a child or two, a man working summers usually. I don't know if you're wanting to sell milk or not, and I don't guess he's got any more money than the rest of us, but you might be able to swap him something. I expect his wife would be glad of some milk, and glad to know another woman is up here."

"Thank you. I will go over there when I can."

"If you can get the way back to the Oberfield Road, you'll find it all right, it sits on the east end almost to the Ruckel Junction."

"Thank you."

He lifted his shoulders. He put his boot in the stirrup and raised himself up on the horse in that clumsy-looking way, maneuvering his wide leather chaps. She stood below him, looking up, still holding one hand over her eyes.

"You've made me think of it, Mr. Whiteaker. Please take some milk with you." She went in the house again. She had left the pans of milk cooling on top of the wooden kitchen box and on the little table. At the smell of the milk poured out into the mason jar, the orphaned calf bawled tiredly.

She went out again and held the jar up to him. His face had gone bright-colored. She was slow figuring out what he thought, then she reddened a little too.

"For the pie," she said. "And the calf."

He ducked his chin and finally took the jar from her. "I haven't had any in a while," he said, not looking at her. "I make a pretty good bread pudding when I've got the milk for it."

"Please come and get some whenever you like." She said this last with some stiffness, a formal sound. He had annoyed her, believing he might be expected to pay.

She stood with her arms folded on her chest. "Well. Goodbye, Mr. Whiteaker."

He looked away. He said, low, "If you need anything, we're not far off." Then he turned his horse out of the yard. She stood and watched him. He looked back once, when he had got almost

to the edge of the trees. She lifted one hand. He returned her
wave silently, in a short clumsy motion, holding on to the milk
jar and the reins with the other hand.

# ❀ 12 ❀

*14 April (Sunday)* It has been cold and no rain, the puddles frozen
at Night. I have leveled the floor in here somewhat with a spade
and strewn it with saw chips, hope it will dry out now, and let
me have a place to stand not in mud. Also sewed up a Ticking
and filled it with boughs & green tips blown down on the wind,
and the smell of the wood & the boughs is sweet and clean.
Otherwise did not work today, I don't know if from Devoutness
or Dullness. Had a bath as well as I could, the water hot anyway
and clean but for the twigs that come down on the creek while
the pail fills. Made a poor job of my hair singlehanded standing
in the Tub and pouring water over from a pan, but it was done
After a Fashion. Also read the nwsppr that was left behind with
Mr Whiteaker's dried apple pie, tho the news was of last Winter's
wheat prices, and wrote a letter tho I know it won't be posted
soon. And so had a Day of Rest. My hair has not dried entirely,
I hope it will not freeze overnight.

**13**

A woman rode out of the trees and stopped at the top of the hill to let down the fence rails. Blue saw her before Tim did.

"Look," he said.

Tim was sitting on the ground behind the calf, pulling back on the top leg with both hands, pushing the bottom leg the other way with the hook of his boot. He looked at his horse first, standing on braced legs holding the rope tight that kept the calf's forelegs from too much squirming. Then he looked over at the dogs facing off the anxious cow, holding her frozen by the straight stare of their yellow eyes.

"No. Up there."

Tim looked up the hill. Then he dropped his look to the calf. "Do it," he said. "I'm getting tired of holding him."

Blue pulled down the calf's sac until it was tight, slit the end of it with his knife, pulled out the testicles one at a time and cut them from the cord. Then he turned a little, lobbing the testicles toward the clean can. For a moment he stood up straight. He cast a sidelong glance toward the woman. She was coming down across the grass slowly on a big black mule.

"Come on," Tim said. He was still sitting, holding the calf.

Blue bent down for the iron. The end of it was pink and he dragged it across the grass a couple of times to cool it. Then he bent over the calf's hip and pressed the iron against the hair. The calf bawled, holding a steady drawn-out note as long as the iron touched it. Tim let go the calf after that and it stood wobbly, slinging its head, looking around. Blue waved his arms. "Yo, go on," he said, and the calf staggered off along the slope toward the cow.

The woman had come up in the yard by then. She sat very straight on the mule, watching them solemnly. She had a wide mouth and she held it in a flat, firm way. Blue's own grandmother had had a look like that. He thought it wasn't stubbornness, exactly, but a sort of staunchness.

"Mrs. Sanderson," Tim said. He shifted his feet, turning side-on to her without seeming to know he was doing it. Blue saw he was gathering himself for a stiff little introduction. "Mrs. Sanderson, this is Blue Odell," with a slight flapping of his hand in Blue's direction.

"How do you do, Mr. Odell." She nodded once, appraising him quickly under cover of the little movement of her head.

He nodded too, and smiled slowly. "Hello, Mrs. Sanderson," he said.

"I have brought the branding iron," she said after a moment, looking at Tim again.

"Well good," he said. He looked over at Blue and then back at her. "We just started," he said, as if there was a point in that, though Blue didn't see one.

The woman made a small adjustment of her position, maybe she sat up straighter. She had coffee-colored hair tied up in a small knot at the back of her neck and then the loose fuzz of it clamped down under a limp man's hat. The coat she had on was a man's too, with the greasy cuffs turned back once or twice. She got down abruptly from the mule. Her big plaid skirt was tucked up in some way to ride astride, but she got that undone with a little tug on it and then she pulled a branding iron out from under the fender of the saddle. It was wrapped up in an oily rag against rust. She unwrapped it deliberately and stood silent, waiting, with her hands holding the CrossTie brand. She was tall, her shape inside the big coat all long bones, like a boy not done filling out yet.

"We could use a front-end man," Blue said, after he'd waited long enough for Tim to say something.

Tim looked over at his horse, then down at his boots. "Yeah," he said. He got up on the bay, signed to the dogs, started out to the little knots of cattle. They eddied away from him gently as he walked his horse among them.

Blue stood not very near the woman, both of them watching Tim and the dogs. She didn't ask him anything. In a while he glanced toward her. He said, "We been using the horse for the front end, but we mess up a lot of brands with the calf flopping around. The work goes better if we've got somebody to put a knee on the neck and hold the calf real flat so it can't squirm."

She cast him a sidelong look. Then she said in a formal way, with her eyes fixed on the calf Tim was bringing down, "Thank you, Mr. Odell."

Tim let the dogs do the hard work, cutting a calf away from its mother, and then he came in and dropped a rope on it, towing it bawling behind him while the dogs held off the cow. When he swung down and walked out along the taut rope to the calf, the woman went out quickly too, fumbling clumsily to get a hold on the forelegs as Tim took hold of the tail and a rear leg. The calf twisted as it flopped onto its side, the front end landing hard and late. Tim didn't look at her, didn't say anything. He got around behind the calf as he had done before, sitting pulling apart the hind legs. The woman pressed a knee onto the calf's neck and then wriggled around some, pursing her mouth, getting her other knee and both hands to hold the two front legs still. When Blue set the brand against the hip, the calf bellowed softly, straining his eyes with fear.

Blue had never got to feel comfortable with cutting the sex out of a calf while a woman watched. He turned and came at it a little backward so the woman might not see around him to what he was doing. From there, with his hindside to Mrs. Sanderson, he gave Tim a look. Tim kept his head down.

"It works easier, sometime, if you take hold of the ears with one hand and the behind leg with the other," Blue said gently, without looking at the woman. "They don't fall quite so hard."

She nodded her head without speaking. Her face was set and pink, holding the calf flat.

When she went out to the next one, she took it by the ears and the behind leg and dropped it neatly. Her mouth was straight. But she rubbed her cheek against her shoulder and Blue saw her hiding the little flash of satisfaction.

When they started, fog was standing up like a cockscomb on the roof of the house and lying along the ground under the trees and in the hollows. But gradually the sun began to burn a hole in the overcast, showing pale at first behind the thin cloud and then growing slowly harder and yellower. The wind shifting blew the black soot and sting of the branding fire. When the woman got hot and put off her big old coat, Blue could see the outing flannel dress was resewn from another size — there were pale lines of wear and picked-out stitches showing in the bodice and the long narrow sleeves. Shortly there was blood on it and mud and short hairs and little burnt holes. While they waited for Tim to bring a calf up, she would stand with her arms down and sometimes rub her palms against that filthy skirt. She kept from picking at the little spoiled marks on it. Blue got hot too. Dust and hair were in his nose and mouth, itching inside his shirt. His back and his collarbone ached.

Every little while a cow would charge the dogs and come mad and bellowing down the slope after her calf. The first time it happened, Blue was squatting, pulling at the calf's sac. Tim yelled and jumped for it, and Blue, jumping too, had a glimpse of the woman's face, cutting a look to the side, making sure before she ran that they were both running too, and only then letting go the calf, bolting behind the piled-up firewood with her dirty skirt belling out around her boots.

When they had got all the CrossTie calves doctored, Blue

watched Tim for a Quit look, but he kept on silently, doggedly, bringing up Half Moon calves after that, glancing at the woman from under his hat when he thought he wasn't caught at it. He didn't say anything to her about fairness.

Finally Blue said, "I could eat." He looked at Tim as they stood away from doctoring an ugly brindle bull calf. The woman straightened slowly with both hands pressing against her back. Tim was still bent over, working his hand under his chaps to finger his bad knee. In a bit he stood and kicked a stump piece of fir wood in the fire.

"We've got those corn dodgers," he said, looking at Blue. "And we've got beef."

Blue knew what he was getting at. They had been saving the testicles up. Tim would strip the sinew out of them and fry them up in lard. *Mountain oysters.* But he didn't want to cook them for Mrs. Sanderson, there was no telling how she would feel about eating them.

Tim looked at the woman finally. "The dodgers are getting pretty old by now, I expect you'll need to wash them down."

She made a small movement with one hand and smiled in a funny flat way, widening her mouth out a little. "I'm hungry enough, I don't believe I'd complain." She looked from one of them to the other.

Tim nodded. He rubbed the palms of his hands across his shirtfront. "Okay," he said, and he went off toward the house. Blue stood awkwardly next to the woman. Finally he made a gesture with one bloody hand. "I'll heat some wash water," he said. He went after Tim into the house, leaving the woman standing alone in the yard with the dogs.

He stirred up a little fire in the stove, started a kettle of water to heat, rummaged around to find a thin slip of soap, a towel that might have been clean, a basin they generally used for shaving their whiskers off. He laid it all out neatly on the bench. He and Tim didn't speak at all. Tim was straightening up the mess in the house with jerky nervous movements, pulling blankets up on the narrow beds, scraping old food off a stack of dirty plates, kicking litter up in a drift in the corner. Then he went to the door.

"Come on in if you want," he said, sounding not like himself, soft and timid.

The woman came inside. Blue saw her look, taking it all in without seeming to. He couldn't tell by her face what she thought. Tim nodded to her once and went right out. Blue, after a moment, said, "Take your time, ma'am," and then he went out too, leaving her alone for a private toilet.

They went down to the pond, walking slowly, holding sore bloody hands out from their sides. They didn't say anything. At the edge of the bank, Blue squatted and rolled up his shirt sleeves one turn and stuck his hands in the cold water. He got his hair wet too, combing it back with his fingers. He rinsed the short itchy hairs and dust out of his mouth. Tim had taken his shirt all the way off, was washing himself with slow care. His upper body looked dead white, with a sunburn line at the neck and around his wrists. Blue stood behind him, rolling his damp sleeves down, looking at the pink puckered scar on his back where the horn of a cow had taken him a couple of years ago.

"She's the one who took Claud's place at the Jump-Off Creek," Blue said, without the need to make it a question — it was plain enough. Tim didn't say anything. "She holds down her end pretty good," Blue said after a while. Tim kept washing. Finally he made a low grunting sound that might have meant yes.

They went back slowly to the house. "Maybe we better give her a little more time," Tim said, not looking at him. They stood around in the yard and Blue smoked a cigarette. He watched Tim sideways, but he couldn't tell what was wrong with him. The dogs lay on their bellies in the shade of the house, watching both of them.

Then they went cautiously in. She was pulling her skirt down, maybe, with her back turned to them. She stood quickly straight and came around facing them, smoothing her palms against the folds of dirty flannel. She had drawn her hair in a little, repinning it, and her face was clean, the skin of it looking tight and shiny. Maybe some of the dust and cow hair had been shaken out of the plaid dress. She had washed her hands but there was still black around the nails and in the lines of her fingers and palms.

Tim nodded and went past her silently, back into the cool room half-dug into the ridge behind the house. Blue, left alone with her again, looked around the room.

"Sit down, ma'am," he said, when he thought of it.

The woman sat in the rocking chair they had got out of old Loeb's place when he died. She didn't rock in it. She sat still with her rough hands loose in her lap, her face solemn, tired. Blue made the coffee, dumping out the old grounds and starting over. He cast around for something to say. "You're doing fine, ma'am," he said.

He could see he had surprised her. She gave him a wide look. "Thank you, Mr. Odell. It's hard work."

"It's hard, ma'am. And we've got too few of us. It gets a little better when there's a full crew and a decent set of corrals."

She nodded gravely. "I can see a use for five or six of us anyway."

"At least that. I've been on ten-man crews and we stayed busy. We were branding two hundred calves a day, though."

Tim came in again with a big flat piece of meat he'd sawn off the carcass of the cow hanging up in the cool room. He went to the stove and banged things around. No one said anything. When Blue looked at the woman, she wasn't watching either of them. She was staring out the window at the trees, her face slack, unguarded.

They ate quietly, looking down at the food. The dodgers were cold and stale, but Tim had split them and spread the grainy tops with the little honey they had, and that helped them down. The shoulder meat was tough, but he had dragged it in meal or crumbs, salted it pretty good, fried it in fat. The woman didn't seem to mind chewing it. Blue watched her face when she drank her coffee. She drank it slowly, looking down into the cup.

In the afternoon they switched off. Tim let the bay horse out and Blue saddled the roan and did the roping. He found he was nervous, making the first cast of the rope with the woman watching him. He was afraid of catching the rope under the roan's tail, or around his neck, like a clumsy kid. But he made the catch all right and after the first one he didn't think about her anymore. He thought about how many calves they had left. He kept looking over at them while he was holding one down, to see how many they had to go.

It was Tim who called Quit in the afternoon. He just stood up from a calf and said, "It's getting dark." There was a lot of light left and calves too, but Mrs. Sanderson had a ways to go to get home. She sighed, not arguing, straightening her back slowly. Blue was sore too. He pulled the brands out of the heat and stood looking down at the fire, shrugging his shoulders gently.

"I make a pretty good onion pie," Tim said to the woman. He said it as if he thought she might argue. "If you want to stay and eat again." He wasn't looking at her.

She made one of those odd quick smiles, turning it on each of them. Blue saw why it looked flat: it didn't show at all around her eyes, it was just a movement she made with her mouth. "Thank you. I believe I'll start home while there is light."

In a moment she nodded as if they had said something else. "Thank you," she said a second time. Then she started across the grass after her mule, walking slowly, rubbing the heels of both hands against her skirt.

Tim watched her and then he turned and went back toward the house. Blue picked up the woman's coat where she had left it dropped on the ground and he carried it out to her. Maybe she had remembered the coat herself. She rode the mule at a walk down the slope toward Blue, smiling slightly in a gentler way.

"Thank you, Mr. Odell."

He handed the coat up to her. "Sure," he said. Then he said, "If you want to stay and eat, one of us would see you home."

She made a small pulling-up motion with her shoulders. "The fact is, I am more tired than hungry." She said it tiredly, plainly, so that he felt no need to answer. She put her hand down suddenly for him to take. "It was good to meet you, Mr. Odell."

He shook her hand. It felt narrow and hot. "Thanks for helping out," he said in a moment.

She nodded seriously.

"I guess you ought to take that brand home," he said. He went back and got it for her. He cooled it in the dirt, wrapped it up and handed it to her. She held it across the saddle.

"Thank you," she said and smiled again and turned the mule out. Blue watched her ride off slowly through the bunches of cows. When he turned to start down again to the house, he saw Tim had come back out in the yard after the can that had the mountain oysters saved up in it. He looked once toward Blue, or toward the woman who was letting down the fence at the top of the hill.

❖ 14 ❖

The mules sounded the warning with silly plaintive brays. Lydia's body had made the bed warm. She waited, lying rigidly where she was. Then the goats took up bleating and there was another sound, perhaps one of the mules, an indistinct grumble like a complaint. She surrendered the quilts and got the shotgun from under the bed, found the paper box of shells, sat on the edge of the bed in the darkness fumbling a shell into the breech of the gun. The air was cold. Her fingers were stiff and swollen.

She came out of the house and around the corner of it to the edge of the brush fence, shaking in the cold dark wind. The goats never would be kept in by the brush fence when determined to get out, so she had lately kept them tied at night. They went jerkily back and forth on their ropes, crying pitifully. The mules had come down near the house. They kept away from the goats, standing high-headed and eyeing whitely across one another's shoulders. Lydia stood watching them and then watching up the hill. There was a thin low moon but it was black under the trees and the wind made the long shadows shake. There was nothing to hear over the loud bawling fear of the goats.

She went a little way along the edge of the line of brush, up the steep hill toward the trees. She held the gun in both hands, shaking, putting her bare feet down with care. She had had the gun from her mother's brother when she was thirteen. She had killed a lot of things with it, snakes and sage hens and hares. Once a coyote. It had been a good gun once, a handmade L. B. Settlemeier with an engraving of pheasants on the breech. But it had been used badly before her uncle got it, the mahogany stock gouged in a couple of places and the finish worn off, the barrel pitted from poor storage. Sometimes now the hammer stuck. She doubted it could kill anything of size — almost certainly not all at once.

She didn't go very far up the hill. Her knees were shuddering, rubbery, they wouldn't take her. She stood at the edge of the trees peering uphill into the blackness, clenching the old gun in both hands.

"Hey!" Her yell came on an outbreath without her quite knowing that it would. The sound was high and short and hoarse, it got something to move ahead of her, a heaviness. She stood still, only her heart lurched. She was afraid to shoot the gun, then it would be empty. She stood still and waited, staring madly against the dark.

"Unh," it said, and moved, she heard it move through the fence, pushing the brush down or out of the way. The blackness shuddered, there wasn't any shape on it, just a spasm, and that sound of something going heavily through the fence. She stood still. After a long time, she backed away down the hill toward the house, sliding her feet along the ground. She went down along the fence to the corner of the house and put her back against the wall and stood there holding the gun and looking up into the blackness under the trees. The wind was cold. Her shoulders, her knees shook; presently her teeth rattled too. She stayed where she was, pressed against the hard log wall of the house.

Brush broke again but it was not the fence, it was farther over on the hill. She stepped out from the house and held the gun up, but she couldn't see where it was. Nothing came down out of the trees.

Little by little the goats gave up bolting back and forth on the ropes. They stood as near the mules as they could reach and fell into an uneasy quiet. When they had been still a while, Lydia went into the house. Quick and shaking, she put on Lars's big coat, stuck her bare cold feet in unlaced boots, got the box of shells and went out again. She stood there at the corner of the house where she could see the trees and the hedge and the goats. She held the shotgun in both hands in front of her, with the shells in the pocket of the coat.

The mules and the goats gradually became unafraid. They may have slept, shifting their weight from foot to foot. She stayed where she was standing near them holding the gun, waiting for the slow, cold daylight. Nothing moved again under the trees except the wind. When the sky became colorless, limpid, she went carefully up the hill and found the big bear's prints in the soft duff, so that what had seemed dreamlike hardened suddenly and became actual.

She heated a little water and bathed her dirty feet before dressing slowly, standing close to the stove. Her eyes stung. She pushed her knuckles against them. Behind the lids she saw the black heavy thing moving in blackness going across the way in front of her — how close — ten feet? Her heart beat slowly, but she heard it inside her ears.

She let down the goats and put the milk to cool and ate a little mush and afterward, slowly, went up the hill behind the house. She took the shotgun and carried the box of shells chinking lightly in the pocket of her coat. She followed the marks the bear had left in the soft ground going across the hillside. They were plain for a while and then not. She hunted for them patiently. The bear had started off north. She kept that way, only wigwagging a little east and west to catch the trail if it had veered. She found a track again, northwest, going down the hill. And then along the trail beside the Jump-Off Creek there was one plain print going off toward the North Fork. She stood and looked at it, holding the shotgun down in front of her with two hands. She went back and saddled the black mule and rode after the bear. She had no clear idea what she meant to do.

After a while, in the mud next to the trail, the bear's tracks swung west, and following them she came down to the North Fork of the Meacham by a rough, straight way. The trail beside the creek was beaten flat and wide in hardened old mud; the only marks showing on it had set there after the last heavy rain. She looked for a little while without expectation, then gave it up.

She thought of going over to Tim Whiteaker's. *I have had a bear after my goats. I wondered if you had had him around here at all.* When she could not get it to sound unafraid, she rode the mule back along the Jump-Off Creek and home and afterward, for two or three days, slept poorly with the loaded shotgun on the little rug below the bed.

# ❀ 15 ❀

The trees left off at the bottom of the hillside where the rails cut a pair of straight lines beside the old toll road, and in the open basin the station buildings squatted behind the long rows of stacked-up fuel wood. There were half a score emigrant wagons parked along the slope above the creek, winter-overs, who'd more than likely soon be moving down to the gentler valleys of the Willamette. They looked mute and sodden and sightless behind their puckered-up storm flaps. All of the people in them were Johnny-come-latelies, trailing forty years behind the big emigrations, and maybe they knew they'd find opportunities poor now, two years into the depression.

Below one of the tailgates, a woman crouched on her haunches. She was heavy, with lank earth-colored hair. She held a wailing child against her while she bellowsed a wet-wood fire.

Danny said, "They should've started down to The Dalles by now."

In a moment, though he was indifferent, Jack answered, "Maybe the river's too high."

"They should've started by now." Danny looked away irritably from the woman, along the dark ruts of mud that bisected the valley. Maybe the low, wet, fishbelly sky and the crying baby and the woman's smoky fire had put him flat. He had gotten prone to low moods lately. Jack thought his humor might improve when he'd had a beer, and some folding money in his pocket where he could reach and touch it with his hand.

The three of them unsaddled and turned their horses in the

stock pen and hauled bundled hides on their shoulders as they crossed through the mud to the store. The clerk, Greevey, was alone. He raised from his penciling to study them in the oil-lamp dimness.

"How-do," he said. "Get you boys beers?"

There was a long trestle table cramped among the trade goods in the little room. They dumped the hides down on the floor beside the table, sat along its benches and blew on their cold hands. Jack went over the four bits change in his pants, selected a nickel, put it out on the table with the others. Then he touched the beer glass lightly with his fingertips. It was cold. There was a cold frost on the glass.

"Looks like she's gonna rain again," Greevey said. His mouth fashioned a careful, self-reproaching smile. He smelled faintly of dampness, and brewed coffee.

Danny fingered out the list from an inside pocket. "We've got eleven wolf hides and nineteen pair of ear," he said. "Also two fox and one wolverine. We'll want these things to buy out of the money we got coming."

Jack set his emptied glass down. There was a white scum on the inside of the glass and a greasy mark on the rim where his mouth had touched. He wiped his wet mustache with the edge of his hand and put out a little more of his own money.

"You got eggs?" he said. "It's been a while since I've had an egg."

Greevey held the list between his thumb and forefinger, squinting at it and then squinting down at the pile of hides. Finally he put the list down flat on the trade-goods counter and went off to rummage the egg and crack it frying on the little cast iron stove. While he watched the egg, he put his index finger against a sideburn and smoothed the bristles carefully.

"Them hides look pretty thin, pretty patchy," he said.

Harley made a sound as if he thought that was funny, but he didn't smile. He had a habit of snorting like that, without ever letting it get to be a smile. Jack looked at Danny.

"We been bringing the hides up here for half a year," Danny said. Jack could hear the little wheeze that started whenever he was tired out or mad. "I guess we thought you'd be glad for the business."

There was red by now in Greevey's neck. In a moment, without turning around to them, he said, "Well, I got some bad news for you boys, you see, and I was hoping if you had some good hides there, well it'd take the sting out of it. Because the state, they've dropped their bounty. These are hard times you know, boys, and they just ain't able to pay out all that money no more and they've had some gripes anyway about beeves and sheep killed to make bait and little kids and dogs accidental eating the poison and whatnot, and they just dropped it altogether. Maybe next winter, they say, but for now there ain't no more bounty. I was hoping them eleven hides you brought would be good winter prime stuff, because those sets of ears you've got are no damn bit of good to either one of us today, and I'm damn sorry about it too."

He ran out of impetus at the end, dribbling out the last few words gently, apologetically, and then busying himself through the silence by getting Jack's egg out, sliding the plate across the gritty boards of the table, hunting up a fork, a saltcellar, a mason jar of red-pepper sauce.

Danny lifted his head, looked at Jack. Jack looked away. He wiped his sleeve against his mouth and stared across the little room to the sooty corners, where crates were piled up against the walls.

Harley made a coarse and bitter sound. "Well that's just bejesus fine," he said, in his low, muttery, mad way. "They cut the legs out from under us just like that and leave us setting in the mud on our goddamn butts. That's just bejesus fine and dandy." He ran the words together in a long complaint, his furious look fixed on Greevey.

Greevey spread his hands apologetically. "I know, boys, I know, but I got nothing to do with it, nothing at all. Listen, I'll tell you what, I'll give you the best price I can on them hides there, and then I'll cook up some more eggs, they're on the house, plate of eggs for each and every one of you, on the house. You know you boys ain't the only ones left holding an empty sack over this. There's been half a dozen cowboys in here the last couple three weeks expecting a payday on their ears. I tell you, it's been hard as hell on me to break the news, hard as hell. I could've just put up a sign outside, you know, done it that way cold as a witch's tit, but I felt you boys deserved to hear it from me. We been doing business a good long while, like you said, and shit, you deserved better than a sign nailed on the wall, that's the way I felt."

Jack left the egg. He pushed back his end of the bench and went out through the stacks of goods, away from Greevey's endless wheedling speech, out to the porch where it was raining now on a slanting wind. He sat on the edge of the porch and chafed his hands together. He could hear Harley's voice again, not the words through the log walls, but a hissing sound of bitterness.

They had reason to bitch: a whole damn season's work gone for nothing. Eleven no-good hides. When Greevey got a good look, they'd be lucky to get a gold piece for the lot.

In a while the other two came out. They stood near him on the porch and stared out to where the clouds pushed down against the tips of the trees.

"Shit," Danny said, low.

They stood silently together and finally Harley cleared his throat. "I don't ride the grub line," he said. His face was red in blotches. "I'd sooner steal than beg." As long as Jack had known him, he had had a strong dislike of riding the grub line. Maybe he had been made to eat humble pie once, or maybe he was just holding on to some conceit.

Danny looked at him. Then he came down off the porch. He stood in the mud with his hands in his coat, and his hat brim dribbling rain. He looked at Jack. "I guess I'll go over along the Snake and look for a job. You coming?"

Jack bunched his shoulders coldly under his sheep-hide coat. He didn't know what kind of an answer he could make. "Greevey pay you for the hides?"

Harley blew air through his mouth in that humorless sound of bitterness. "He stole those hides is what he did."

Danny never looked at him. He dug out a coin and sailed it across to Jack.

Harley said, "You can live high on that for half an hour."

Danny looked toward him but didn't say anything. Then he looked at Jack and pulled his hat and went heel-sucking through the mud to the horses. He slid the saddle over on the horse's back and rocked it gently and reached under the belly for the cinch strap. Jack watched him unhappily. Finally he left Harley standing alone on the porch and he crossed to the pen. The rain was thin and cold, blowing up from behind him, wetting his neck. He stood next to Danny, watching him.

The two of them had lately talked: when they got their money this time they'd go down along the Snake, where there were still some outfits that didn't fence up much, were still working the old way, with a full spring roundup and a fall drive taking steers to railhead. The wolves had been pretty much cleaned out, and if they could get on for the summer somewhere, and put a little away with the wolfing money, they could maybe put up in a town the next winter. Maybe at Nyssa. When Jack had been a kid he'd got on tight with an outfit on the upper Snake, spent four or five years on that spread. Got deflowered down there too, by the only whore in Nyssa, a lady he remembered even now for her long white legs and long hair colored pale as straw. Jack had begun to think a lot, the last few weeks, about the Snake country and those old times and that whore he had loved once. But now the ears had come to nothing and the hides would hardly buy newspaper to line his leaking boots. He knew, with a sudden certainty, that he'd get down there and there'd be no jobs and too many ahead of them on the grub line and the Nyssa whore dead or deadly, and in a while the memory of that old time would get sucked dry. But that wasn't anything he could say to Danny.

"We're flat busted broke and no prospects in sight," he said finally. "Cowboys out of work all over the state. You want to ride the grub line? We never done it up to now."

Danny looked off across the basin. Maybe he was remembering something, himself, something to do with better times. "I guess I'll try a few places before I go to the grub line," he said. Then he put his boot in the stirrup and swung up on the horse.

Jack hunched his shoulders, squinting up through the rain at him. "We got a roof where we are," he said. "We can keep on there like we been, if we got meat. I don't figure it's stealing if a man shoots a cow when he's hungry."

Danny looked annoyed. "I guess if the cows was ours," he said, wheezing, "we'd think otherwise."

Jack looked away, and then back. It had always irritated him, this business between Danny and Whiteaker and the Indian. "They wasn't never no friends of yours. You said they weren't. Stuck to themselves, you said."

Danny squirmed a little on the saddle as he looked off toward the line of trees against the overcast. "I guess they were just minding their own business."

Jack wiped his whiskers. "Well, I'm staying. You staying with me?" he asked finally, irritably.

Danny tightened his hat down. "No," he said. "I guess not."

He touched the horse with a spur and turned him along the ruts of the road. He went past Harley, standing on the porch under the eaves of the store. The kid looked at Danny, and then down at the boards under his feet.

Jack heard Danny say a couple of words. "Snake," he heard. The kid didn't say anything. Jack didn't either.

And then Danny was gone on away from them, following the road. It went ahead of him, out of sight in the trees along the brim of the basin. Jack stood in the rain watching him leave.

"Shit," he said, but without moving his mouth much, and the kid probably didn't hear it. There wasn't any heat in it anyway.

**❖ 16 ❖**

There was a woman in the yard, pinning overalls and towels to a line strung between thin, leaning maple trees. She looked and saw Lydia and stood away from the laundry line, wiping her hands on her apron. There were two boys playing in the mud. When they saw where their mother was looking, they jumped up quick and went inside the house. From the far end of the wagon lane, Lydia could not tell how old they were. Under six?

She came on slowly on the black mule lately named Rollin. It seemed to take a long while to get across the grass with the woman standing there watching her come, and then hard to tell at what point she ought to call out a hello, or stop the mule and wait to be asked in. She felt a little rigid smile fixing itself on her face.

"Hello!"

"Hello!" The woman's face was flushed, or windburned. She had a pressed-thin smile she was holding too. "You are the woman at the Jump-Off Creek," she said finally, so that it was not directly a question.

"Yes."

She nodded. "Mike met Tim Whiteaker out on the trail lately and he said you would be coming." The woman was big, her arms and neck thick through, her face wide and round. She was still very young, that wide face as smooth as a girl's, and above it a mass of brownish hair shot through with streaks of fading girlish blond. She kept it braided and pinned up on the crown of her head in a big neat coil. If she had let the braids down she would have looked about sixteen. She was, maybe, twenty.

Lydia sat on the mule, smiling stiffly. Finally she said, "I'm Lydia Sanderson."

The woman nodded again. "I'm Evelyn Walker." Her hands twitched at her apron. "I'm real glad you've come. There's no women up here hardly. Come in, won't you, and I'll get us some coffee." She sounded formal, unpracticed.

Lydia stood self-consciously off the mule, pulled her skirt loose, smoothed her hands against the bunched-up wrinkles. She had wrapped up the jars of milk in towels and set them in saw chips in a hamper carried across the front of the saddle. While Evelyn Walker watched, she took the hamper down. She left the mule saddled, only pulling out the bit so he could get at the green grass. "I have brought a little milk with me," she said. "I am trying to find a few people to trade for it, if I can, as I often have more than I need." She had made up her mind to say that much quickly, before politeness had got in the way of the business she had come on. She smiled determinedly.

Evelyn Walker's face became pink. She lifted her own hamper, piled up with the unhung wet clothes. "We had a fresh cow ourselves, once," she said, as if she had been asked about it. "Mike bought it off a family going East on the La Grande Road. We were getting better prices for the cattle then and we had the money. But she has since died and we haven't had the extra to buy another one." She lowered her head suddenly and then raised it. "When Mike comes in I know he will want to get the milk. He'll know what we can trade for it."

Lydia nodded, standing where she was holding the heavy hamper. She found she had not ever lost her narrow, rigid smile. She wanted to say something about the narrowness of her circumstances, but nothing came.

Mrs. Walker got the door of the house open and held it with her hip for Lydia carrying the milk in. There was just one long room inside, with a curtain that could be pulled across to screen one bed from the other, but the logs on the inside of the house had been planed so they lay flat as boards and then two walls papered and the last two painted clean with whitewash. The windows had been hung with bleached-out sacking embroidered finely along the hem, and there was a little table overspread with a red silk scarf, and on it two painted figurines and a blue figured bowl. Out from one of the papered walls stood a good small stove with a damper on the smokepipe, and an oven box. In the small clean house Lydia felt a vague melancholy, not like tears at all but like the emptied out tiredness afterward. She widened her smile against it.

"Where have the children gone, Mrs. Walker?"

Mrs. Walker set the laundry down, waved both hands vaguely, smiling. "Oh, they're hiding under the bed. They don't see anybody but us, usually, so they have got a fear of strange faces. Junior! Charlie! You boys come out from under there now. Come out." But when they didn't come, she let them stay where they were.

There was a kettle still sitting on the stove from the washing just done. Mrs. Walker lifted it off and set it on the floor and then got out a coffeepot and a grinder. "Oh sit in this chair, Mrs. Sanderson, it's got a better seat. Do you like toast and jam? I have a thimbleberry jam, you know the berries are very dull just to eat but they cook into a good jam."

"I'm sure I would like it."

"Please don't notice the bread. I've never got this little stove to bake bread without burning it."

Lydia kept smiling purposefully. "I hope you won't mind if I do notice the bread, or the smell of it anyway, as I do like that already." She had a proneness to sound stilted, mannered, with other women, she knew it herself. Sometimes in other women's faces she could see that she was taken for pompous and she glanced toward Mrs. Walker for sign of it. Mrs. Walker's face was pink, both her hands were at her chest.

"My mother used to say she liked a sharp-set guest, they will eat whatever you put out and praise it though it's poor." She kept the palms of her hands pressed against her bosom, not looking at Lydia and then looking at her with that flushed face. "I'm very glad you've come," she said, quick and low.

She dropped her hands, wiped them on the front of her apron. "Here, we won't wait for the coffee, we'll have toast right this minute, don't you think, we can have the coffee after."

She set the toast out on good white plates, brought a small pot of blackish jam and sat opposite Lydia in the chair with the broken cane seat. She used the tips of two fingers to push the jam pot slightly toward Lydia. "Please do eat as much as you like."

They each spread jam on the toasted bread and ate a few bites in polite silence.

"Mr. Whiteaker told Mike you were homesteading all alone." Mrs. Walker lifted her flushed face. "I'm afraid I'm just full of questions about that. You must stop me if I begin to ask too much, or sound like an old Paul Pry."

Lydia shook her head, looking down at her hands. She felt a little heat come up in her own face. "The truth is, there is not much interesting about it. You'll be soon bored."

Mrs. Walker's face became intent. "Until I was sixteen and married, I lived in my father's house in Alicel, down in the Grande Ronde, and since Mr. Walker and I have been married I've lived in this little house and I believe I've never once gone anywhere alone but berry picking or fishing and that within a loud yell of a man, so I daresay I wouldn't be bored with hearing how your life has been different from that."

Lydia could not help a small laugh, or the way it sounded, sharp and sour.

"The fact is, I have never lived anyplace before this but my father's house. My husband just brought his things and moved into my room when we were married."

Mrs. Walker's look became pinker. "Oh I'm sorry," she said, in a flustered way.

Lydia could think of no response. It was not clear to her what Mrs. Walker felt sorry about. She thought she wouldn't say anything else, but then a little more came out into the silence. "When he died, I sold my husband's clothes and his dog and horse and everything that belonged to him, to have the money to come West." She heard the tone of her own voice, without any grief, heatless and stiff, and was surprised, herself, to feel a sudden itchy need for sympathy, or for forgiveness. "I suppose his mother is rolling over in her grave," she said, in the same flat way. She picked up a slice of toast, bit it, chewed dryly.

"Oh I'm sure not," Mrs. Walker said finally, on a low let-out breath.

They looked at one another. "I only think there must be a deal of courage in you," Mrs. Walker said slowly. "If Mike were to die I don't know what I'd do except to go and try to find myself a new husband to take care of me and my children. I couldn't ever stay here by myself, it'd be too lonely and too hard. How do you sleep without anybody against your back? The nights up here are so black and full of the sound of varmints you can't see. And how will you ever get the man's work done on that place? You are quite as thin as six o'clock."

Lydia smiled dimly. "I don't like the nights," she said. "But I'm not afraid of the work. I kept up the man's work on my dad's farm for fourteen years. He was sick from the time I was twelve, in bed most of the time and always calling my mother to tend after him so it fell to me to do his work. I was the only child of theirs that lived, there wasn't anyone else to do it and keep us from starvation."

Mrs. Walker shook her head vaguely, seriously. Then she smiled. "Oh Mrs. Sanderson, you see I'm not bored yet!"

She stood and got the coffee off the stove, holding the handle of the pot with a bunched-up corner of her apron. She poured it into china cups. Lydia brought a little milk out of the hamper and sweetened the coffee with it.

"I don't know what Mike will say about the milk," Mrs. Walker said in a whispered way.

Lydia looked into her coffee, stirring it. "I'm sure whatever he decides, I will think it's fair," she said, with slow, unavoidable embarrassment.

They sat at the little table and drank coffee slowly in a tender silence. Eventually the boys scraped their heels restlessly against the floor under the bed, and one of them hunched out from below the edge of the Wedding Ring quilt. He sat up close to the bed, with his thin small body drawn up in a bundle and his face half hidden behind his arms. Lydia looked at him gently, slowly. After a while the other boy came out and crouched next to his brother.

"Junior is three," Mrs. Walker said, looking toward them without moving her head. "Charlie is two or will be in a month."

"They are pretty boys, both of them."

She flushed. "I think they are," she said, pleased. She brought her chin down so that, like Junior, her face was half hidden behind her raised arms holding the coffee cup. "I had another one, a girl, born first," she said in a lowered voice.

Lydia looked away. After a while she said, without knowing she would say it, "I have carried two, but could not keep either of them past the third month."

Mrs. Walker gave a little clucking sound, soft and distressed. After a while she said, still low, flushing brighter pink, "I'm carrying another one right now."

They passed between them a brief, private look.

Into the long silence afterward, Lydia said, "Your clean clothes will be dank and cold, laying there in that pile. I'll help you hang them, we would be done in a minute."

They went out together, standing next to one another in the cold spring wind, pinning things by the shoulders, the waist, to the long sagging line.

"I guess there are little blessings," Mrs. Walker said. "There is only your own things to wash when you're living alone."

"I don't believe Mr. Angell had a place to hang his laundry at all. He cut down every tree around that house, there is no place to tie a line. I've been just laying things out on the twigs of bushes."

Evelyn Walker nodded. "When I came here, Mike didn't have a line. I planted these trees, they're wild things from the woods, and put a line up the first week I was here." Then she said, looking sideward at Lydia, "That place of Mr. Angell's is in a sorry way, I guess. I haven't seen it, but that's what Mike says."

The two boys had come slowly out from the house. They squatted next to the door, watching Lydia from behind their pulled-up knees. She looked back at them. Then she looked at Evelyn, and at the big man's shirt she was snapping out in her hands. She felt a slow, surprising intention.

She said, looking at the shirt, "My dad never said a good word to me all the time I was doing his work. I believe he was ashamed of what I was doing. He got Lars Sanderson to marry me, I heard that afterward from more than one person, and when I asked my dad, he wouldn't deny it. He wanted a man to be working the farm, and Mr. Sanderson wanted a farm made over to him. I guess he didn't mind me as a wife, as he knew I always had worked hard and without thanks for it."

She heard the shake coming into her voice, but she kept on with what she had decided to say, only beginning to smile a little, helplessly, feeling it stiff and askew on her face. "When he dropped dead, I sold about everything he had brought to our marriage, even the ring he had married me with, and I came out here to Oregon. I don't know who's taking care of my dad's place now, and I don't give a damn either, except for my mother's sake."

Her hands too were shaking by this time. She took a child's shift out of the wet pile and snapped it twice. "The truth is," she said, "I'd rather have my own house, sorry as it is, than the wedding ring of a dead man who couldn't be roused from sleeping when his own child was slipping out of me unborn."

She hung the little shift silently, pinching the pins down hard with the fingers of both hands. Her face felt red and stiff. She had not ever told that much of it to anyone.

After a while Evelyn Walker, from where she stood beside her at the clothesline, reached for her hand clumsily and squeezed it. When Lydia looked toward her in embarrassment, she saw that Evelyn's eyes had filled with tears. "Oh, Mrs. Sanderson, I believe we will be wonderful friends. I've just been beside myself with loneliness, and here you are, lonely as me!" The girl made a wordless sound and took Lydia in a short, fierce embrace.

It had been a while since Lydia had cried over anything. She was surprised when a few dry tears squeezed around the edges of her eyes. But it was the lost babies, she thought, and could not be loneliness, that made her feel this quick, keen need of Evelyn Walker's friendship.

## ❖ 17 ❖

*6 May* Have got the soil dug up a little and on the dark Moon will put down on Mrs. Walker's advise potato eyes, onions, beets, parsnips, turnips. Had hoped to grow corn at least and shell beans but her luck w them has been poor, the Summer too short to bring them on, so I will not try them or not this yr. It was slow tilling, the ground woven thru everywhere with roots of the trees A. had sawn down. Could not get the plow down in it much. Some other Spring I must burn out the stumps but for now make a crazy Quilt of small odd plots knowing the poor potatoes will take odd shapes as well. I am desperate in need of some green thing, beet tops or the young onion pulls, as I have had little besides corn mush and the goats cheese since coming to this place.

O I have shot a Rabbit today and on the day before caught a Trout in the Jump-Off Creek with a worm in a mud ball! Planted a squash vine at the corner of the house which if it grows I will train up the roof edge, as I have no flower seeds & the squash will look pretty there and do double work. My Health is good, and my thumb which was sprained at Mr Whiteaker's in the branding is healing at last, the swelling gone out of it so I can hold a hair brush now and get my hair done up decently as I have not for a week. I find I have the company every little while of a man or a boy who is Riding The Grub Line. (I have this from Mrs Walker.) I am so far off the road it is always a surprise to see them come into the yard but they know of the houses that are vacant, the word goes around among them. When they see this house is not empty any longer they generally stand hat in hand and ask a meal for a wood-chopping or "whatever needs done". If they will settle for milk and cheese of which I have plenty I do not turn them away Hungry, only one boy for a rude manner and a man who said he could not abide milk, it gave him red bumps. For the most part they are quiet company & soon gone, for which I am glad enough, and in any event glad to have wood cut by hands more idle than mine. I believe the white goat Rose will kid in the Summer tho the man who sold her swore she was just Fresh & not bred. O well she will be Fresh again by Winter and I suppose I cannot starve as Louise gives more than I can use, every day without complaint.

# ❀ 18 ❀

Tim sat up in the darkness and reached for his pants.
"What the hell."

"I don't know. Something after the horses maybe. I heard one of them, right before the dogs started in."

They didn't make a light. Tim went past Blue struggling in the dark to button his pants, reached high to the five-point rack above the lintel of the door, and brought down the first gun his hands touched, knowing it by the feel, passing the Marlin back to Blue who was standing now at his elbow. He reached up again for the Miller. In the darkness, sightlessly, they counted the loads.

They went out to the porch, each taking hold of a dog, hauling scruff of neck back into the house, pulling the latchstring through to shut the dogs inside. The frenzied barking kept up, coming muffled a little from behind the door.

Tim looked over at Blue and then out across the fenced field where the horses were standing in a nervous huddle away from the trees. It was dark under the trees, flat blackness. He had already made a pretty good guess what it was, from the noise the dogs were raising. They didn't generally bark much, they'd been trained away from that. And they'd gone crazy but they hadn't left the yard; they hadn't gone that crazy. So he figured he knew. Blue would have made a guess too. But neither of them said anything.

They went bare-soled across the wet grass, past the horses to the edge of the evergreens.

"We ought to have brought a lantern."

"Yeah."

They stood listening a moment, and then Tim said, "We'd better let him know we're coming."

"Hey!" Blue said, loud, quick. Tim felt the muscles jump in his arms.

They went carefully into the blackness beneath the trees. In the darkness, barefoot, Tim stepped gingerly, holding his rifle in both hands. The bottoms of his feet itched with cold and the thorns of trailing blackberry vines. He couldn't see a damn thing, could hardly even make out the dark bars of the tree trunks and the horizontal line of fence cutting across in front of them. His head felt light, trying to listen. He heard the slight draw of his own breath, the springing of the ground under his feet.

At the fence they found where the bear had broken down a rail and gone over into the forest. It was too dark to see anything else.

"Long gone," Tim said, but for a while they stood waiting, looking up the little slope into the trees.

"Well hell, I'd better go back for a light," Blue said finally. He looked at Tim. Then he started back. Tim saw him break into a trot, going across the grass under the starlight.

Tim waited alone, standing beside the fence line. He kept his back to the house, kept looking out under the trees. He listened but he could only hear the faint sounds of the dogs crying from inside the house, and the horses not settled down yet, blowing air. As he stood still, waiting, he began to shake a little with the cold. He hadn't put on any shirt over the thin cotton undershirt. But his hands holding the rifle were warm, sweaty.

Blue came back across the grass, walking long strided inside the swing of yellow lantern light. He carried the Marlin in his free hand, not resting it across his shoulder or in the crook of his elbow. He had let the dogs out, and they sprinted across the grass ahead of him, silent now, and stopping along the fence to anxiously smell and pee where the bear had been.

In the light from the lantern Tim and Blue found the sign and squatted to peer at the bear's prints there in the soft ground.

"Shit," Tim said. The hair had risen along the back of his neck.

"Big grizzly. Pretty damn big grizzly," Blue said.

Tim touched one of the prints with the tips of his fingers. There was a little dark dribble in it, maybe it was blood. "He might have a bad foot."

"Leg-hold trap."

"I bet. Maybe he chewed out of it or muscled it open."

They fell silent, standing looking out at the trees. Blue slapped the front of his undershirt looking for tobacco. Not finding any, he leaned against the fence and then stood up straight again, finally bent and fiddled with the lantern, trimming the flame a little.

They had had a couple of run-ins with grizzlies before this. Once along the Sprague River when they were with the Crazy W a bear had come through the roundup camp and killed a horse. A little man named Weedy, or Wiley, had lost half of his face — one eye and an ear, all the flesh off his cheek. Blue had been sitting right next to him before the bear came in there. He'd killed it with a shotgun at about six feet.

In a moment Tim said, "Maybe we ought to run him down tomorrow."

Blue looked over at the dogs. Then he looked at Tim again, smiling slightly. "The dogs don't look too happy with that idea."

In Montana they'd had a boss who raised dogs just for running bear, and ran bear just for the hell of it. They'd seen him bring in a big grizzly once. He was short three dogs when he came in, but happy as hell about that big hide. He had a bitch at home throwing new pups and he didn't give a damn about those dogs he'd lost. Right after that, they had quit the outfit. Maybe Blue was remembering that.

Tim shrugged. "Hell," he said, looking away. "I'm not too happy about it myself." But he was. When he looked at the prints, a prickly excitement crawled up the back of his neck and sang in his scalp.

Tim said, "If he wasn't gimped and mad, he'd probably go on over the Umatilla, maybe he'd go up to the hot springs and raise hell with those bathers who come east from Portland."

Blue looked toward him, not finding anything funny in it. For a while he didn't say anything. Then he said, "Maybe he's going up to the high ground. He might not be that stove up. He might go up into the Wenaha country."

Tim touched one of the dogs as it came and stood alongside

his leg. He bent a little and ruffled its yellow coat. "Maybe," he said.

Blue held the lantern down again, close to the prints. "Shit, he's big," he said. His eyes shone in the light.

In the morning they left the dogs behind and followed up his trail. He had gone away to the northwest, not fast. Probably he was lame, but in the daylight there weren't any dribbles of blood in the prints.

They trailed sign as far as the beaver marshes above Lick Spring. The way was bad there, sticky mud under a scum of green with a lot of old timberfall and close standing brush so they had to pull the horses long-necked behind them through the brake. The bear found the low way, on four feet, his puddled paw prints going along almost straight beside the muddy edge of the marsh.

They didn't follow him very far in.

"I don't know," Tim said. He stood half under the neck of his horse in the close space and waited for Blue to come up behind him. "He's bound to come out of it on the north or the west, that's the way he's been going all day. We could go around and pick him up there, it'd be quicker."

Blue made a wordless sound of agreement, but he said, "If we don't pick up the sign along the other side, we'll lose him."

Tim looked up briefly to the low overcast. "It's about to rain. We're liable to lose him anyway, then."

Blue shrugged. He didn't say anything else. He backed the roan out slowly through the brushwood until it opened up enough to turn around.

"I wondered how far you'd follow him in there," he said. "Only a damn fool would follow a bear into that scrub."

Tim shook his head. "Shit. You followed me in."

The horses shied suddenly, bumping together. Tim heard the roan horse make a little sound, and then Tim could smell it too, or hear it, or just know it like the horses, and he tried to get the bay to come around, skittering, so he could grab for the rifle in the saddle boot. He got hold of it but then a horse's heavy butt wheeled and knocked his teeth together and he was on the ground watching the bay taking off through the brush, kicking high sheets of mud. He scrambled around on his belly, half under the roan's feet, Blue's feet, laying his hands on the rifle again. Blue had hold of the roan's forelock and one stirrup, dancing with him, pulling at him to come around. Tim on his knees saw the red stripes in the roan's belly, the horse's legs scrabbling rubbery, disjointed. Blue kept hold of the roan's forelock, kept after his gun, his boots in a puddle of the horse's blood, yanking to get the Marlin out from under the fender of the saddle. Tim found the bear in the notched sight, he knelt slippery in the wet with the muddy rifle up against his cheek misfiring twice, three times, while across the sight he followed the big flat face, open-jawed, grinning solemnly. He only saw from the edge of his eye the one arm swinging wide, brushing Blue off the ground and then letting him down like the roan horse, wobbly. The last two hit dry enough to fire. A sudden neat red hole appeared in the bear's cheekbone below the right eye. The head ticked back slightly, briefly; when he opened his mouth, gouts of blood came out with the low sound, the sigh.

Tim kept kneeling where he was, waiting, starting to shake. "Blue."

"Yeah. Christ."

Tim put the gun down in the mud and went, shaking, across the bloody wallow on his knees.

"I don't know," he said stupidly, kneeling over Blue.

"Christ, you blew half his head off." Blue lay on his belly with his cheek against the mud. "It's okay," he said after a while. "I'm okay. He just clipped me. Those damn horses. Listen, Tim, I don't think old Jay is dead."

Tim stood and walked wide around the bear to the long-legged roan horse. Jay's tawny eye watched him come up. He took the Marlin off the saddle. The stock was cracked. He stood holding it, waiting a little bit, breathing through his mouth until his hands stopped shaking some. He shot the horse once behind the ear and then went back to Blue. He knelt on the soft ground, rocking back on his heels, putting his hands flat on his thighs. The horse, or Blue, had stepped on his hand. He sat looking down at the purply slow swelling.

"Blue."

Blue opened his eyes. "Those damn horses," he said.

"I got to tear your coat."

"No, hell. I can get out of it."

"It's rent anyway. Just let me cut it."

"Well, hell."

Tim put the blade of his knife to Blue's coat and sawed it up the middle of the back, that and the red shirt, laying them open tenderly. Blood ran down and puddled in the mud. Tim took off his own jacket and unbuttoned his shirt. It was his right hand that was sore. He worked the buttons slow, wrong-handed.

"We must be ten miles out, twelve," Blue said. His eyes were closed again.

"Not that far."

"The hell."

"The bay won't go too far."

"The hell he won't."

"I'll find him. I got no plans to carry you on my back."

He folded his shirt a couple of times until it made a long pad going out into the sleeves. He laid it against Blue, against the sheeted blood. "Can you suck in your gut so I can get this tied off?" He pushed the sleeves up under Blue, knotting the shirt around him. Then he put on his jacket again over his bare undershirt and squatted there thinking.

"What the hell," he said. "I guess I'll give you a ride. I got to move you out of here."

Blue kept his eyes closed. "I figured I'd just wait where I am."

"It's pretty wet right here," Tim said. Then he said, "You'd draw more bone-pickers than a cemetery. You're laid up next to a lot of meat." He waited, then he came around in front of Blue and put his hands under his armpits.

"Christ no, just give me a hand. I can get up." Blue took a couple of long breaths. He pushed with one hand, rolling up on his side, drew his knees up like a kid, pushed on his hand again to come up to a sit. "Christ," he said, letting his breath out.

Tim looked away. His belly was sour, aching. He looked at the big body of the bear, the bright place where the blood ran on the grass.

"Here," he said, reaching his good left hand down to Blue. Blue took his hand and Tim pulled him grunting to his feet. He kept hold of him. He leaned in against him, bracing. "Okay?"

"Yeah. Wait a minute. Yeah."

They went a couple of feet, scuffling.

"We'll be here all night," Tim said. "I'm gonna carry you."

"Yeah. Shit."

Silently Tim bent and levered him across his shoulders belly down, crosswise. Blue made a huffing sound. Tim struck out through the brush, staggering a little, whistling breath in through his mouth. He put Blue down against a windbreak, a rotted cedar, clear of the thicket. The ground was spongy, there wasn't any drier place.

"I'll go back for the gear," Tim said. Blue leaned sideways against the log. He said something, maybe it was *okay*, without moving his mouth.

Tim went back for the saddle and gear off the roan, and the empty Miller rifle, the broken Marlin. He lugged it all back and piled it next to Blue, put the stinking saddle blanket over him, leaned the loaded Marlin against the stacked-up gear. "It's got a busted stock," he said.

Blue made an irritated grimace. "I paid forty dollars for that gun."

"It's not broke. Just the stock."

He didn't move to go yet. He looked out into the trees, silently nursing the sourness in his belly, holding his sore hand clasped in the good one.

"I guess my smokes are done in," Blue said.

Tim went back to where he had left the bloody shirt lying in the mud, went through the pockets for the tobacco sack and the papers. There was blood on the papers but some of them, the ones on the bottom, were okay. He brought the stuff back and Blue made a slow, careful cigarette. His hands looked steady. Only there was blood drying in the palm lines and between the fingers of his hands.

Tim bent and unbuckled his chaps and let them drop there on the ground.

Blue began to smile, as he smoked and watched him through pinched narrow eyes. "Planning a long walk," he said.

Tim shrugged. "Don't go anywhere until I get back."

"I'll wait. A nickel says that horse beats you home."

"I'll catch the horse, but hell, you won't be able to ride him."

"You know I never have been so stove up I couldn't ride. You taking the nickel bet?"

"Hell yes. I'll be back with him shortly."

He walked off through the trees, east. The bay had left plain marks on the ground. He followed them. When Blue was out of sight behind him he broke into a jog. If he ran part of the way, and if his knee held up, he thought he might cover the ten or fifteen miles by nightfall. The horse was on a beeline for home, he knew that. He'd catch him along the fence line above the house, and get the little steady dun of Blue's, and then he'd have to find the way back in the dark, in the rain. And pay up the nickel.

He ran and walked, ran and walked. It started to rain softly. He walked up the ridges and ran down them, skidding long marks in the duff digging in the heels of his boots. When he smelled smoke he veered off toward it, a quarter of a mile before he came over the hill and saw the boy there at the tail end of a supper stop, wiping out his tins, stowing his gear to move again. It was Turnbow's friend, Osgood, the redheaded kid with the big hat. There was a stiff hide showing flakes of dried blood, rolled behind the saddle of his horse. It didn't look like wolf — maybe it was badger, though badger wouldn't be worth much.

Tim waited, leaning over, letting the rain cool the back of his neck. He felt his heartbeat fast and hot in his bad hand. He waited and thought about it until some of his breathlessness had tapered off. Then he went down limping through the trees toward the kid, hallooing when he was still a ways off and then coming in more slowly. The boy watched him a minute, standing stiffly beside his horse with his hands hanging pale and long-boned below the too-short cuffs of his shirt sleeves. Then he booted mud on the fire and pushed a toe in the stirrup and mounted up. He sat on the thin pinto horse waiting for Tim to come.

Tim said, "You saved me a couple of miles."

The kid was wearing his closed-up look. He waited without saying anything, seeming to study the backs of his hands.

"Lost my horse," Tim said. Then, not what he meant to say, "I'm in need of one."

The kid pulled his Adam's apple up and down his long neck. In a low, breaking voice, he said, "Where's the red nigger?" and Tim's belly rolled.

He put his hot right hand against his pants leg. He had been running quite a while, his knee was swollen, on fire, if he'd had a gun he'd have stuck it up under the kid's nose. What he said wasn't what he'd thought about saying when he had stood on the hill making up his mind to come down. "We were tracking a bear lamed in one of your own damn traps. I expect you all just walked away when you saw the sign, and left it for us to finish."

The kid's face got blotchy around the pimples. He gave Tim a quick, careless look. "Well then finish it," he said, low and hot.

He touched his horse to move. Tim reached for the bridle and the kid's boot shot out and took him on the cheek, ramming teeth against the inside of his mouth in a starwheel of brightness. He had his fingers on the headstall, he held on to it. The horse jerked backward, startled, lifting him on his toes, and the boot swung in again, hit him hard in the chest, under his heart. He didn't think he'd let go of the horse, but his back hit cold and wet against the ground. When he got a little sharp breath back in his chest, he heard dimly through the buzz of pain the horse carrying Osgood off through the trees, not hurrying, leaving Tim alone there with the rain dribbling against his face, running with the little trickle of his blood.

## ❖ 19 ❖

The mule made a sound that woke her: a single homely bray. She did not lie waiting for its repeat but pushed her feet down in her boots and took the shotgun across the black room to the window, to the barred storm shutter and the peephole giving on to the south edge of the brush fence. The rain had ended for the moment. The two goats moved darkly, silently, on the part of the slope she could see. She watched them. A dim bouncy light came up slowly onto the hillside so the goats began gradually to cast long shadows.

"Ma'am."

It was Tim Whiteaker's voice. He said it not very loud, or from a distance away, around at the front of the house.

She went to stand behind the door in the little light that came between the unchinked logs. She held the shotgun down in one hand and with the other hand held together the front of her bed dress. "Yes, Mr. Whiteaker."

He said, "Can you come," or something like it, the words furry, run together. He might have been drunk, there was something of that sound in it, but she could not stand behind the closed door in case he was not. She did up the buttons on her wrapper. He said, "Ma'am," again but that was all, waiting for her.

She pulled back the bar and came out under the eave of the house into his lantern light. She was still clasping the shotgun in one hand. He sat on a horse in the yard, hunched up under his hat as if it were still raining hard. The light of the lantern he was holding up cast him in strange black shadow.

"Can you come," he said again, and when she did not answer he ducked his head. "Blue needs stitching up."

"All right." She nodded. "Wait."

She went in again and dressed, tied up her boot laces, pushed her undone hair under her hat. She put needle kit and carbolic in a handbag and toted the saddle out from where she kept it inside. The man had gone around behind the house. He was trying to get hold of the black mule, walking it into a corner of the brush fence, arms spread wide. He had set the lantern down on the ground and in its high light he looked jerky, clumsy. The mule kept away from him.

"Here," she said. She went past the man gently and up to the mule, leading it by the rope hackamore. Mr. Whiteaker stood lamely with his hands hanging down, watching while she lifted the saddle on. She saw there was mud or blood on the front of his coat, a big mouse beneath his right eye, a little streak of dried blood there where the skin had split.

When he saw her looking he shifted his weight anxiously. He bent down for the lantern and, carrying it, raised himself with stiff care onto his horse again.

On the mule she followed him back along the Jump-Off Creek. The lantern cast a high jumping light, long jumping shadows.

Ahead of her the man sat his horse tenderly. He looked slight, thin as a shadow himself. Someone — Blue? — had lately given him a neat straight haircut, had shaved the back of his neck below the hairline so it looked smooth and white and unprotected.

The dogs ran out to them when they passed through the fence, trotting out stiff-legged and then smelling the man or seeing him and shifting to simple seriousness. Mr. Whiteaker rode past them without a word, rode up to the door of his house and hung the wire handle of the lantern on a nail at the eave of the roof. He tipped himself rigidly out of the saddle. He looked at Lydia, a sliding sideways look, and took hold of the mule's bridle.

"Go on in, ma'am. I'll put up the animals." He went off into the dark, pulling the horse and Rollin behind him, while she took the lantern down off the nail and carried it inside the house. The Indian, Mr. Odell, was laid out on his belly on one of the two narrow beds. He squinted his eyes against the glare of the light. His eyebrows seemed thick black marks drawn across the pallor of his skin.

"Oh, Mr. Odell."

He made a little smile, not moving his mouth much. "It's okay, ma'am," he said in a low voice, hoarse. "I been worse."

She scraped the bench up next to his bed and sat on it, with the lantern held up in one hand to get a look at his back. She had sewn up cows and goats — once her own thumb. But raw wounds made her qualmish on the first seeing. The fine hair lifted along her arms, a light hum rose and sang in her head.

"Barb wire," she said in a doubtful way.

"No, ma'am, I guess not. We jumped a bear."

She nodded. "Oh, I feared that," she said, with the intention of not sounding fearful at all.

She stood and took off her coat and hat. It was hot in the small room, doubtless it had been Mr. Whiteaker who had earlier made the fire in the stove. She saw he had set water to heat there as well. She brought the kettle over to the bench and with a wrung-out towel began to daub away the drying blood, the threads of shirt in the long wounds. She felt the man holding still, grinding his teeth — Lydia not being his wife, mother, sister, he would not yell, could not complain. She was tender, but pitiless, having never gained pity and so never learning it. She painted his back with yellow carbolic and began to stitch closed the several shallow furrows. He kept his eyes closed and his breath came sometimes harshly from his mouth.

"I'm sorry, Mr. Odell," she said once, without stopping what she was at.

He opened his eyes and closed them slowly. "It's okay," he said, in a breathless sort of way.

When she was finished she drew the edge of his blanket up to the back of his neck. The wool smelled of sweat and staleness. "All right," she said.

He made a rough sigh, that was all, without opening his eyes. She sat on, watching him sleep. Mr. Whiteaker never came inside. Finally she took the lantern and went out and found him leaning against the wall of the house in the darkness.

"Mr. Whiteaker."

He stood somewhat straighter without standing away from the house. "You got it done?"

"Yes."

He nodded. He seemed to think something over, then he said, "I appreciate you coming out at night like that." He mumbled it, perhaps around the soreness of his face.

"Of course."

He looked at her. "I'd have done it myself," he said, mumbling still. "I've sewed him up other times. But a horse stepped on my hand. I couldn't hold on to the needle." He lifted his right hand slightly so that she saw it was swollen, discolored.

"Have you broken it?"

"No. I guess not. I just couldn't hold on to the needle."

She nodded, accepting this information the second time without comment.

He looked at her again, and away. "We started a bear," he said.
"Yes. Mr. Odell said so. Have you killed it?"
"It's dead."
In a moment she said, "I have had one after my goats."
He nodded again, not surprised, said, "He had a lame foot,"
as if it might be an apology.

It had been hot inside the small house, the air outside felt
sharp, strengthening. But it was too cold without a wrap. She
began to shiver. "Come in, Mr. Whiteaker. I believe I ought to
take a stitch or two there below your eye."

He looked down at his boots. "It'll close," he said.

She waited for him without replying. Finally he stood away
from the house. "All right, ma'am," he said, and followed her
into the house.

He sat on a chair staring past her while she cleaned the little
cut and tacked it closed. The eye above the wound was swollen
narrow, blood-veined, it watered slightly when she pushed the
needle through the skin. The watering eye or the sour man's
smell of him made her think suddenly of her dad. The skin of
Mr. Whiteaker's face was coarse, stubbly, like her dad's too. But
when she stood back from him she saw Mr. Whiteaker again, that
childish expression he had, like a boy holding a stiff smile against
his will.

"Shall I look at your hand?"

He looked down at it and then held it out. There was a bruise
and a swelling on the back of his hand, the fingers looked stiff
and swollen too. She touched the lump lightly.

"I don't believe it looks broken."

"No." He dropped his hand, let it rest on his thigh. She saw
him look sideways cautiously at Blue. The Indian slept heavily,
sweating, with his mouth open slightly to let out his harsh breath.

"I'll sit up with Mr. Odell," she said.

Tim Whiteaker ducked his chin. "I don't mind seeing you back
to the Jump-Off if you're wanting to go home."

"I'll sit up with Mr. Odell a while."

He nodded. "Well," he said.

"You look quite spent, Mr. Whiteaker. Please lie down and sleep and I'll wake you when I'm ready to leave."

He nodded again, not arguing. He went to the other bed, a low log frame holding a mattress on crosspieces of rope. He sat on it and took off his hat, pushed his left hand back through his cropped hair. Then he lay down on his back with his sore hand cupped on his chest. He didn't try to get his boots off. He looked at the ceiling a minute and then closed his eyes. After a while he made a little sound, it might have been a word.

"What," Lydia said. But he was quiet after that, asleep.

In the turned-down light of the lantern she sat in the rocking chair without rocking. Her eyes burned in the close dry heat. She heard the dogs settling restlessly under the house and once after that a cow lowing in a mournful way, but chiefly what she heard was the unaccustomed sound made by the breathing of the two men, hoarse and regular.

She woke suddenly, jerking up in the chair. She had dreamt a little, a short jumbled dreaming of her dad, and it had been Lars, in the dream, who woke her. *Get up*, he had said, pushing his thumb against her side. She hardly remembered his face now, after three months, but in the dream it had been distinct, a wide face, pale eyes, and the thick lips like a woman's, with strong sculpted curves.

When there was enough light she stood and went quietly out and home on Rollin without waking Mr. Whiteaker, there being no reason to do so and several for letting him sleep. She was glad enough to get away from the oppressive, crowded little room, the smell of blood and illness. Her dad's room had always smelled like that. Her mother smelled that way too, carrying it on her clothes, the pores of her skin, into other rooms.

**❖ 20 ❖**

It wasn't as if it was a bad time of year for one of them to be laid up. They had turned out the cows and were at the point of making new fence, cutting brush. It wasn't anything that couldn't wait.

"I can get up on a horse," Blue said, sullen, arguing with no-body. He got out of bed to piss and afterward went back to bed. He flopped around restlessly and sweated and swore and looked at Tim sidelong in embarrassment.

"You shuffle," Tim said, and got out the deck of cards. They played monte, not speaking of anything except the cards. Blue lay on his side of the bed, propped up on an elbow and a pillow, wincing when he leaned out to play his cards.

"Christ, I can't win," he said, after the third hand, or the fourth. He pushed the cards together irritably. Tim looked away. He stood and rattled the stove until the fire caught. "I guess I'll do a wash," he said.

He heated water and went around piling up dirty clothes. Blue watched him without speaking. Tim did the wash slowly, systematically, in hot water and soap suds, with the big kettle set on the low bench. He gave over the wet things one after the other for Blue to do the wringing out, his own hand too bruised to squeeze anything. Then he went out and put the clothes to hang on the fence where it ran close behind the shed. He did that slowly too, smoothing the shirts and the socks with his fingers. The sun was out. The wet clothes, smelling of soap and water, steamed a little when he lifted them out of the tub.

He went inside again. The house was hot and damp. Blue slept on his belly with the blanket pushed off him so Tim could see the black tracks of the stitches in the yellow flesh. His face was slack, he breathed noisily through his nose.

Tim went out. He sat in the shed, rebraiding a rope until his hand started to hurt. Then he came in again, limping on his sore feet, nursing a sore mood. He lay down on his own bed. His feet hurt, and his hand, his face. He lay a while without sleeping. Then he sat up and got his Miller off the rack and put a handful of shells in his pocket. Blue kept sleeping. Tim went softly out and dragged his saddle from the shed and caught up the bay horse. The dogs wanted to come. He left them standing in the yard, looking after him sorrowfully.

He didn't know what he meant to do. But he rode up toward Loeb's place, carrying the Miller across his lap, resting his sore feet lightly in the stirrups. In the trees below the park he stopped and sat in the saddle looking up toward the little shack. There were a couple of horses there cropping the grass, one of them was the rib-thin pinto that belonged to Osgood. If he had meant to front the boy the intent went slowly out of him now, leaving a sour, peevish fretfulness.

After a while he rode out of the trees into the high and windy sunlight and deliberately across the long slope to where the horses grazed at the ends of staked-down old ropes. No one came out of the house. Without planning it, he cut the rope from the pinto horse and softly drove it down the grade into the trees. It was a small horse with a short choppy-looking gait. There was mud on its butt and the coarse tangled tail. He pressed it into a trot down the long wooded mountain. His chest felt tight, airless. But gradually, driving the horse ahead of him, not thinking at all about where he was headed, the tightness passed out of him and he grew more or less happy.

The pinto was not happy, being pressed. When the bay pushed him, he laid his ears back and bared his yellow teeth. But he went on where he was driven. Tim never let him stop to feed, only at the bottom of the long mountain he let the two horses stand and drink in a nameless stream that ran north. After that he kept them headed north along the creek bottom. The weather was bright and warm and when the wind fell off in the afternoon, it grew hot even under the trees near the water. The sweat under Tim's clothes made him itch.

Eventually, without deciding to, he brought the bay up next to the pinto, pulled one boot out of the stirrup, jabbed the pinto with the rowel of his spur, low and hard along the horse's stifle. The horse made a quick piglike sound, a kind of squealing snort, and broke into a gallop, cranky and kicking. Tim kept the bay held in. He watched the pinto until it had run out of sight up the creek, toward the Umatilla River. Holding the Miller under his clamped-down elbow, he took off his hat and wiped out the sweatband with his handkerchief and rubbed his sleeve across his itching, sticky forehead. Then he resettled the hat and started back for the Half Moon. It wasn't until then that the enjoyment began to go out of it slowly, and the thing that set in was a kind of discomfort, like embarrassment.

# ❁ 21 ❁

18 May Weather good finally with sun and a light wind, cold night and morning. I have cut poles and nailed them in between the logs of the House and when they have shrunk up I will cawk them with Cement and so have a sound House I hope when the Winter gets here. I wish there was a floor. If I could spare the $ to buy boards I would lay them in now. But no it will have to

be a Punchin floor which will mean no end of work and a steady hand on the froe for which reasons I will put it off until other more pressing things are done. I am down 3FT nearly in the hole for the P. Everyday I dig a little more. I am ready for that to be finished. I have not as much need for Privacy as wish for a good clean Seat. There is a little flower blooming now, it looks very like an evening primrose only Blue, and blooming under the straight sunlite. What a cheering thing it is to look out and see the whole clring Blue as a rug, save only where I have dug up the ground for garden and there the little onions show green tips and I hope the rest will come up soon. Mr Walker came today w 2 loafs of bread frm his wife and took milk when I offered it tho nothing was said of a trade. I wished he could have brought Mrs Walker w him but know she should not come, as it is a long way & steep and no wagon rd to bring her. She sent a sweet note of friendship which Mr Walker handed over w seeming mistrust, I do not know what he objects to, his wife finding a Friend or myself in particular. I smiled and presented myself as ladylike as liable to be with a hammer in my hand & nails in my teeth! I know I will need to make a Friend of him if I am to keep Mrs Walker for a Friend. She wrote that she had made a paste of my buttermilk & cornstarch which her mother had told her was good for chapping & sunburn and the little boys cried when they saw her! Was called away yesternight to sew up Mr Odell who was badly mawled by a bear, by God's mercy or luck not killed. So I am rather more tired than usual, if that is possible, and know that is why I am somewhat downcast tonight and maybe a little sorry for myself. Mrs Walker's dear letter which I know should cheer me has had a contrary effect and I am quite feeling low. It is only tiredness that leaves me liable to these moods, I *shall* be in better spirits when I have slept, I know myself well enough for that, and try to take comfort from it.

# ✿ 22 ✿

When the woman returned, crossing the long clearing to Angell's house, Tim left off the tree cutting. He let the axe down so he was holding it by its head and gave himself a moment before he started down toward her. She was watching for him, he could see that, but maybe not able to tell where the pealing of the axe had come from. He was down out of the trees, stepping carefully around the patchwork of garden, the stumps, wading the shallow creek, before she saw him. She wore a good blue dress and a woman's hat with a short curled brim of soft felt and a gray feather stuck up in the grosgrain band. Her hair under it was tied back neatly in a tight knot so her face looked longer and thinner, bonier than he remembered. She looked not much like the woman who had helped out at the branding.

"Mrs. Sanderson," he said, when he was near enough. He saw she was looking at the place below his eye where the skin had closed in a thin bright-pink line. The bruise there had gone sickly green.

"How do you do, Mr. Whiteaker." She smiled slightly, in the way of a question.

He made a gesture toward the timbered slope. "I've been cutting trees," he said vaguely. He would not quite look up at her, still sitting on the tall mule. In a moment, stiffly, he laid the axe down, took hold of the mule's cheek strap, reached up for the hamper she held across the front of the saddle. She let him take it. But when she had come down off the mule herself she said, "I don't know why you would cut trees on my own property," in a blunt way, and only afterward letting her short smile meeken it a little.

He ducked his chin. "Since Blue's laid up, I ran out of work I could do around there single-handed. I figured you could use a hand."

She gave him an odd look, stubborn or guarded. "You are not obliged to repay me, Mr. Whiteaker, for an act of neighborly kindness." Her look made him want to stand back, as if she had on a coat of long barbed spines. But stubbornly he said, beginning to look away, "I saw you were digging a hole so I dug it deeper. Then I cut some poles, which I figured you'd find a use for, building a fence or a shed or you can saw them up for stove wood." He looked down at his hand holding the hamper. The swelling had gone mostly out of it, it was green-black like his cheek. Then he looked at her again. "I meant to chink the house but I saw you'd already done it."

She kept looking at him with her mouth drawn up small now in that frowning purse. But she did not this time fault his intentions. In a moment she let her mouth out flat again, nodding slowly. "Well yes," she said. He was not able to tell what it meant. She reached out to take the hamper from him. "Come in, Mr. Whiteaker, please. I'll make coffee."

He ducked his chin, flapped a hand back toward the trees. "I got a tree half cut. I'll just go back and finish it first." He picked up the axe and went off around the stumps and the drunken rows of potatoes. When he got to the edge of the trees he risked a look back. She had unsaddled the mule and turned it loose on the short blooming grass with the other mule and the goats and his bay horse. The door of the house was left open but he could not see inside where the woman was, maybe brushing out her dress, laying a fire in the stove.

When he had finished the half-cut tree he went down again to the Jump-Off Creek. He washed his face and hands slowly in the cold water, combed his wet hair back along his scalp with his fingers. Then he put his hat on again so the high white brow might not show above the line of sunburn.

When he tapped the edge of the door, she turned toward him, smoothing her palms along her apron and smiling slightly. "Come in, Mr. Whiteaker. I believe the coffee is about made." She gestured at the room without any embarrassment. "I'm sorry I haven't a chair yet, please just sit on the edge of the bed there. Will you take milk?"

He sat gingerly, balancing on the log frame of the bunk with his hands resting on his knees. When she brought his coffee he held it carefully in front of him with both hands and avoided looking at her. They drank a little in silence. Mrs. Sanderson sat on the camelback of her small trunk. She had blacked her boots so they looked neat and narrow. He kept his eyes fixed somewhere near them.

"I have been over visiting with the Walkers," she said, as if he had asked her that.

He nodded. There was another silence.

"The weather has lately turned for the better," she said, in that purposefully polite way of hers.

He nodded again. "I guess it has." Then, pulling his head down, plunging in, "I am from Nebraska myself, but that was a long time ago."

She gave him a startled look. Immediately, he knew he had bungled it stupidly. He sat staring down at the oily coffee in the cup.

After quite a while she said, without any more point than his, "I came across Nebraska on the train." Then she said, "Do you have family still there, Mr. Whiteaker?"

He had made up his mind to say a couple of things about himself, as a way maybe to get her to do the same. But he had not, until just now, thought of what he might be asked to say. He cast a look along the wall behind her. "I don't hear from them," he said finally. "Maybe they're still there. My dad is dead and my mother might be too by this time." He spoke slowly, measuredly, with a small silence ahead of each thing he said. Still, it felt as if he was blurting things out, saying more than he should, not able to quit. "There were nine of us, it was a big brood. I heard one of my brothers was killed by a horse in the Dakota land rush, that's about the last time I had any news. I been gone from there, cowboying mostly, since I was thirteen."

She sat looking at him silently. He had already said more than he'd meant to. He managed to wait. Then she suddenly gave a little ground. "I came west from Pennsylvania when my husband died," she said. He had got that much from Mike Walker, but now he heard the offhandedness, no old grief in it nor expectation of any sympathy. He looked at her side-on. In a moment she said, "I had notions at the start, of going over to the Willamette country. But I was told by several people that it was very thickly settled and the price of the land very dear." Another quality came in her voice, a flatness, or a resignedness. "My circumstances keep me from those high prices."

He thought about it. Then he said, "We've been up here six years. Everything is pretty well fenced-off everywhere else. And land was cheap up here. We had rode once for a high-woods outfit in the Montana Rockies, we figured we could make a living up here all right." He thought she might understand they were allied. He and Blue had come up into the mountains chiefly for lack of money to go elsewhere, and she had said something like that herself. But she didn't mention it. She said, "Then you and Mr. Odell have been together a long time."

He found he had to think a while to figure out when they had met. "We rode together for Joe Longanecker on the old Rocker S," he said. "I suppose that was twenty years ago." He looked at her again. "We were still raw kids, I guess."

They drank coffee for several minutes after that without speaking. He looked guardedly around the room. The space was dark and small as when Claud Angell had kept it. She had mended

the rusted stove poorly with flattened tin cans, sewn a fresh mattress ticking out of bleached sack cloth, only those small better-
ments and the few womanly furnishings — the high-topped trunk
and a couple of pieced quilts, a framed mirror, a hairbrush, a
little rag rug laid down on the dirt. The floor was swept smooth,
unlittered, things were put away neatly. He wondered if she
wished for an oven-box, a board floor.

"Mr. Odell is on the mend I hope."

"He's getting along all right," he said.

"I believe he ought to have the stitches out by now. Yours ought
to be picked out as well." She stood and got her embroidery
scissors and wordlessly pulled the thread out of his cheek while
he sat there on the edge of the bunk, holding the coffee cup on
one knee, balanced. He looked carefully past her until she was
done. Then he looked down at his coffee.

When she sat again, she said suddenly, as if she were taking
up old needlework and not dropping a stitch, "It was a poor place.
We had some apple trees and a field we usually put to barley and
a kitchen garden that was about an acre." After a silence she said
a second time, "It was a poor place," and then, "The ground was
rocky. We kept goats and sold the milk." She looked at him
straight, but not as if she was answering any question he had
raised. "I did all the farm work there for more than fourteen
years. I am not afraid of work and I'm used to getting by on little.
I believe I can make a living up here all right." She said it in a
dry way, plainspoken, so that he believed her, and didn't feel a
need to say that he did.

She stood and poured him more coffee, then sweet yellow
cream, taking only the cream herself, without coffee. He didn't
know much about her means, just the little she had said and what
he could see for himself, but he figured she would be up against
it this first year, eating poor as Job's turkey by way of making
sure her money and her provisions held out to the next spring.
He had seen enough of that kind of living, had lived that way

himself more than once. She might be glad of an offer out, or it might be her heels were dug in, she was set and single-minded. He figured he knew which it was. He sat looking into his coffee.

"I expect you wouldn't want to try marrying again," he said in a slow way, and feeling the heat come up slowly in his face.

She looked at him. He kept his eyes on the cup of coffee held carefully level on one knee.

"I don't know if we could get along," he said. He looked at her quickly and then away. For a moment the only clear thing he felt and recognized in himself was dread.

"I don't suppose we could," she said after a silence.

He nodded. He rubbed his forehead with the heel of one hand and frowned past her, out the open door across the flat to the wooded ridge. "Well," he said, "I just wondered about it."

She made one of her peculiar brief smiles. But she said nothing else, only sat still holding her own cup tenderly with both hands. Her whole face was bright.

He drank the coffee down in steady long swallows and stood. "I guess I'd better get back," he said.

She stood also, so that in the small room, for the first time, he became aware that she was tall as he was — taller.

"Thank you for the work done, Mr. Whiteaker. Will you take home some milk and cheese." She sounded staunchly polite.

He hunched his shoulders. "No. Thanks. I had the time," he said. "I didn't mind doing it." He went past her, out of the dim, hot little room into the clear bright heat outside. The bay horse sidled away from him, he caught at it impatiently, tightened the saddle, rose onto it. He remembered the axe left leaning against the wall of her house but he didn't get down for it because the woman had come out into the yard by that time and stood with the sun behind her, looking up at him.

"Good-by, Mr. Whiteaker."

He touched his hat. "So long, Mrs. Sanderson."

"You'll tell Mr. Odell that I will come in a day or so to get out his stitches."

"All right."

Her face was pulled up in that frowning squeeze, there was bright pink along the shells of her ears and the thick straightness of her jaw.

He turned the horse out. Nothing was holding still inside his head. He didn't feel anything he could name, except that restlessness.

He was most of the way across the clearing when she called his name. He looked back to see her walking quickly up behind him holding his heavy axe by the head. He thought about waiting where he was but then he started the horse back toward her.

"You left this, Mr. Whiteaker," she said, as if he might have some question about it.

He took the axe from her. She seemed to wait for him to say something but he couldn't get any words to come out. In a moment she smiled in a very stiff way, turned and started back, holding her good blue dress up out of the dirt with both hands. She looked brittle, he could see the wings of her shoulder blades pushing up rigidly under the dress.

He remembered suddenly the time he had quit the Rocking Horse Ranch. He hadn't thought about that in a while. The boss had had a fine wife, she was a big strong Swede with masses of faded blond hair plaited down her back like a girl, and a laugh that was low like a man's but quicker and easier. She and the boss had five or six children. Tim had been maybe twenty years old then, and he had thought she was on her way toward getting old. She might have been thirty, or thirty-five. Both years he was there, she had the hands up to the house for a Christmas supper. He had never worked any place before that where the hands ever ate sitting down with the boss and his family. Afterward, in the parlor, they had all stood around with cups of hot applejack and she had brought out for each of them some thing she'd made and wrapped up in tissue paper — it was peanut brittle candy one year, and the other time a little round hazelnut cake soaked in brandy. She liked to talk, and she managed to talk with each one of them about some personal thing so they would know they hadn't escaped her notice. She asked Tim about the stubborn, bigheaded dun horse he was riding at that time. And about a bone he had broken in his little finger. Whenever she would laugh, he would catch the boss looking at her tenderly over his cup of applejack. The third year as it came around to Christmas, Tim had quit the outfit. There weren't any damned jobs to be found at that time of year and he had come near starving to death before spring. He hadn't known why he'd quit, when he was twenty. But after a few years, he began to know.

Once when he had been pretty drunk he had asked a whore to marry him. And when he had been about thirty, he had ridden a couple of times over to Choteau, Montana, to see a seventeen-year-old girl who soon after had married a logger and moved down somewhere near Missoula. He was forty-one now. He thought, *Suit yourself,* as he sat looking after Lydia Sanderson's narrow back. But there wasn't any great bitterness in it, just a vinegary, helpless discontent.

# ❀ 23 ❀

*9 June (Sunday)* Rode the long way to see Evelyn Walker today, we had a poor short visit, her husband's hired man sick in the barn and she must go back and forth to care for him, and help her husband with the work, the man being too Sick for it. Weather has been hot, if I were Home I would long since have taken the stove down, setting it outside under tarp roof so to cook w/o heating the house red hot. But we are so High up here, nights and mornings are still frosty Cold and I do enjoy the stove then & quilts besides. I am sure Mrs Walker is right about the corn, it would sit & sulk, as indeed the pumpkins are doing which I put in in spite of her good advise. The gray Mule which I named Bill has never put on wt as I hoped, instead got thinner & now has a cough & eats little. I have tried every Remedy and fear the worst. I keep him from Rollin as much as can be. I could not stand long against the Loss of both. Mr Whiteaker has come and cut a score of poles from straight young Pinewood and tho I dislike his Purpose I am glad enough to have them. I have promised myself & the patient Goats I will have a shed & good stout fence before the Weather turns. I know I will be at that work the whole Summer as I am a poor logger and must go a ways to find good trees since A has cut all the ones along the near flat and the ridges are too steep to log. I believe I may use Mr Whiteaker's poles before that, in walling up the Little House, the hole being well dug now & the Seat I have cut out and been planing & sanding in the evenings as the Daylight has stayed longer. I have had Mr Whiteaker's offer of Marriage. I believe the only clear thing I felt on the occasion was Fear, as I have been long getting my Independence and am much afraid of losing it through some Need or Circumstance. If, as I feel, the proposal was forced by Loneliness, I am very sorry on that account. Only I shall not submit to the Tyrant myself, having by long denial learned the value of Self Rule.

# ❁ 24 ❁

There were a few old cows and three horses standing in long shadows on the grass, and a few brown birds on the brown water of the pond. From the fence line above the house she could see neither Mr. Whiteaker nor the Indian, Mr. Odell.

She liked the way their house sat at the foot of the long sloping park, with the little lake in front of it and the steep wooded ridge standing high behind. The house was dark, unkempt, but she admired the cold-cellar and the site and the post and rail fence going around most of the big meadow, and the steep-roofed shed where stove wood was stacked up in long ricks, and tools and saddles had a place to hang out of the weather. There was not a prosperous aspect about any of it, but it looked well established and was soundly built. She set a high value on those things.

The dogs, when they saw her, came trotting out stiff-legged. They never barked. She stayed up on the mule and rode down silently past them, around the edge of the water into the yard. Mr. Odell was under the eave of the shed, hammering nails into a shoe of a brown horse. She hallooed but he never heard her over the tapping of the hammer. Then finally he saw her. He started a little and straightened up and came out a couple of steps into the yard to wait while she rode in.

"Hello, Mr. Odell. I called out but you didn't hear it."

"How are you, Mrs. Sanderson." He took off his gloves, dusting them lightly against his pants leg. His face was wide, all mouth and thick eyebrows, and a heavy forelock of dark brown hair. He had a sweet, rare smile he let out long and slowly: she had liked him as soon as seeing it. He stood unsmiling behind the brown horse, holding on to the gloves with both hands.

"I told Mr. Whiteaker I would get the stitches out for you," she said, not smiling herself.

She saw by his face, he was surprised. "Tim could probably pick them out all right."

"Well," she said. "I am here now."

She had been in an agony of dread, watching the house obliquely for Mr. Whiteaker, but as Mr. Odell reached to take the hamper she handed down, he said, "Tim, you know, is over at Meacham."

She shook her head.

"There is a logging camp has set up over there. We heard they were short a cook. He went over to see about it." He made a vague gesture with the hand not holding the hamper. "I guess we could use the cash. If he gets on there, he can quit in a couple of months when we get busy again."

She said, "Yes," unnecessarily, as she followed him across the yard.

The house inside was hot and dim, smelling faintly of yeast. The top of the table was wiped clean, the board floor had lately been swept.

"Will you just sit on the bench, Mr. Odell?"

He sat on the low bench obediently. She took out the fine scissors, and the tweezers. "Do you want this shirt off, ma'am?" He was watching the scissors with evident anxiety.

"Yes please, Mr. Odell."

He turned his back to her modestly and pulled the shirt over his head and sat hunched on the bench with his elbows resting on his knees. She began slowly to pick the stitches out of the yellow-painted flesh. She felt him holding still, breathing carefully through his mouth.

"You look a great deal better today than when I saw you last, Mr. Odell." She had in mind, in an indefinite way, keeping his attention from the scissors.

"I'm getting along," he said after a while. "I can get up on the saddle, so I don't complain. I guess it wouldn't do me any good." If he was letting out his wide slow smile, she could not see it from standing at his back.

In a moment she said pointlessly, "You have got all the calves branded by now."

"Yes, ma'am. That's done, unless we've missed a few. Rounding up cows in this country is like working a Chinese puzzle. You're never finished with it."

She began to smile, without happiness. "I will have to get used to that. Where I lived, we would walk out to the field and chide them in with a stick."

He nodded in a stiff way, holding still. "I guess I've done some of that. When I was a kid, I worked a couple of years in Clatsop County, it's nothing but dairies over there and flat as a plate."

She had given up, on account of Mr. Odell, several large fancies having to do with the Wild Indians of the West. Now several smaller ones came undone all at once. She had seen, through the window glass of the train in the towns she had come through, a few Indian men and women standing in queues, solitary Indian men sitting on curbstones or walking up a street. Mr. Odell was her only great experience of them.

"Oh, Mr. Odell, I'm afraid I am hard put to imagine you pailing cows."

He may have smiled. He made a low wordless sound of amusement. "It was a long time ago, ma'am." Then he said, as if it bore on the matter, "I never saw a cow dog before I was twenty-five, I guess."

Through the door he had left standing open, she looked for the two dogs. They had gone to lie in the shade of the shed, disregarding her, now that they had watched over her approach of the house. She said, "I have never heard you or Mr. Whiteaker call the dogs by name."

He lifted his head in surprise. "Is that right?" He twisted his head around stiffly, looking for the dogs. "The yellow one is Tag. The ugly brindle is named Hangdog." He seemed to think about it and then he said, "I had horses I named and ones I didn't, but dogs always need a name, I guess."

She said, "Yes. I believe that's true." Then, slowly, "My husband had a hound he kept for hunting but that dog was only a nuisance around livestock."

He nodded. "Well, a dog's got to have the temper for it, and then the schooling." He did not ask at all about Lars.

She said, after a short silence, "I have thought of getting a dog myself. There, I am finished with you, Mr. Odell. And I don't see that I have got you bleeding again anywhere."

He pulled up his shoulders gingerly and sat up straight. "Thank you, ma'am." He stood and put his shirt on before he turned around toward her. "Herman Rooney has a place over on the Five Points. He raises good dogs. Both our dogs came from him." He began to smile slowly. "We had one we'd bought over on the plateau, all he knew about was sheep."

She smiled also, looking down. "If I make up my mind that way, I will get the directions from you, and see Mr. Rooney."

"All right." He looked past her vaguely. "Sit down, ma'am. I'll make up some coffee."

"No. Thank you, Mr. Odell. I believe I'd better go on." She gestured toward the hamper he had set down on the floor beside the platform rocker. "I have brought just a little milk for you, as I had it to spare."

He nodded. "We've been appreciating your milk, ma'am. Tim makes a pretty good bread pudding when he's got the milk for it."

She did not look up from putting away the scissors and the tweezers in her handbag. "Yes."

"I'm putting bread in here for you," he said, crouching over the hamper getting the milk out. "Tim got it made before he left home this morning."

She thought of saying something against it. But finally she said, "That's very kind, Mr. Odell."

He walked out with her, carrying the hamper. She coiled up the string handles of her purse, and looked down deliberately at that.

"Mr. Whiteaker is offended with me, I imagine," she said suddenly. She gave him a short, flushed look.

He turned his face toward her in slow confusion. "I don't know, ma'am."

Then she was miserably embarrassed. She looked toward the sidehill, making a little involuntary sound like a chucking. Mr. Odell continued to walk beside her silently. She could not tell if he watched her. She climbed up on the mule while he stood holding the hamper. When he handed it up to her, she became aware that her mouth was drawn up rigidly. She let it go out flat again.

"Well, Mr. Odell, I'm glad you are mending well." She looked straight at him, smiling slightly. There was still a great deal of heat in her face.

"Thanks to you, ma'am."

She shook her head without otherwise answering. "Well, good-by, Mr. Odell."

"So long, ma'am."

She started the mule back up the slope. She kept from looking back until she stood letting down the rails. He had walked out in the yard to watch her go. She lifted her hand, and he raised his also.

Coming back to the Jump-Off Creek, the trail folded on itself and back again, going over the ridge between Chimney Creek and the North Fork. The way had been a misery in other weather, the trail deep cut with runnels, slick with mud, but it was dry now, hardened in the contour it had taken from the last rain. The mule found steady footing at one edge or the other of the dried-out rills. From the top there was a splendid view east and south to the horizon, the ranks of mountains dark and hunch-shouldered, the steep shadowed gorges parting them. She counted ridges, guessing out where the Jump-Off Creek cut its gully. But from here there were no marks of human society, the trees owned the world.

When she had been fifteen, sixteen, before the hope had worn away, she had used to imagine proposals of marriage, had composed elaborate replies, yes or no, depending on the imagined asker. She couldn't remember, now, any of those unspoken conversations. It had been a long time ago, or had happened to someone else.

## ❖ **25** ❖

When Tim showed up, Blue stayed where he was in the shed, sitting on a sawhorse, whittling at the piece of alderwood he was shaping to a rifle stock. He worked at it slowly, peeling off long thin curls of yellow wood with his pocketknife.

"You're working in the dark," Tim said, coming up to stand at the front of the three-walled shed. Probably there was an hour of daylight left if you were up on the ridges or over on the flat land west of the Blues. But the sun had gone behind the rise of the hills, so it was dusky and cool in the bottoms. Under the cover of the shed it was shadowy.

"I can see," Blue said. He kept whittling. Tim stood just under the eave, watching him. He hadn't unsaddled his horse yet. He stood holding it slackly by the reins.

"Are you cooking, then?" Blue asked him.

Tim nodded. "Their second cook bucked off a horse and broke his hip. They been without one since the middle of the week." He watched Blue a little more. "They shut down on Sundays. I guess I can come up here on Saturday night and then go back down on Sunday night."

Blue glanced toward him, surprised. "It's a long ride."

Tim shrugged. "I can leave there as soon as the last dinner shift is fed. I don't have to do the cleaning up. They've got a couple of monkeys."

Blue looked at him. Then he looked down at the rifle stock. He turned the wood and felt along it with his fingertips in the poor light. When Tim made a movement to lead the horse off, he said, "The woman from the Jump-Off Creek came over here and picked the thread out of my back."

Tim turned and looked back at him. In the dimness, standing at the edge of the shed, his face was featureless, black. "I guess you were on the Jump-Off Creek the other day," Blue said.

Tim kept standing where he was. He didn't say anything. After a long silence, he said, as if he were answering something, "I cut her a few pine poles."

Blue kept waiting, but Tim didn't say anything else. Whatever had gone on between him and Mrs. Sanderson, he didn't mean to tell anybody about it. The bay horse shifted its weight, backing up a step, impatient, and Tim took a step back too, getting away from Blue maybe, and the sound burst out loud, the hard metal echoes wowing off the trees. For a long-seeming moment they didn't move, any of them, as if they had to wait out a sudden little suspension, then the horse's head flung up, startled, eyes rolling white, and Blue came jerkily off the sawhorse, skidding his chin in the wood chips getting flat down on the ground at the back of the shed. He heard Tim flopping down behind the woodpile, knocking loose a little slide of stove wood. Neither of them said anything. They listened to the sound the bay horse made, thrashing his head weakly against the dirt.

In a while Blue said, low, "You got the Miller with you?" One or the other of them sometimes took a gun when they were out working, in case they had a chance to shoot something for meat. Lately, Tim had been carrying his about every day.

"The horse is laying on top of it," Tim said.

So they waited. There were ropy streams of blood squirting out from the nostrils of the bay horse. He made only a low noise, wet, strangling. There wasn't any other sound, except the livestock grunting and shifting nervously. The dogs stood in the yard, wide-legged, poised, looking for something to go after. Blue watched them from where he lay flat at the rear of the shed, waiting. His back began to be sore, from the dive off the sawhorse.

The air got slowly cold and brittle, all the day's heat seeming to go straight up into the clear, colorless sky. Blue had on a thin shirt with the sleeves rolled up to the elbows. He had sweated in it all day. Finally, warily, he got up on his forearms and rolled the sleeves down over gooseflesh, staring out against the failing light.

"He's gone," Tim said after a while. "That was all he meant to do, kill the goddamned horse." He said it roughly, in a sullen voice. Then he stood up.

Blue started to say something but Tim was already standing by then, looking big and bare in front of the shed. Nobody shot him.

"Shit," Tim said, standing there.

Blue stood slowly. His back hurt. He found his pocketknife where he'd dropped it. He folded it up and put it in his pants pocket. He put the alderwood stock piece leaning up against the wall with the hand tools. Tim was pulling his gun out from under the dead horse. When he had it, he walked across the field to the edge of the trees. Blue didn't go. He walked out with a rope and got the dun mare and brought her back to where the bay had fallen dead in front of the shed.

She didn't like the blood smell. He had to go in the house and get some castor oil and smear it up her nose and then she stood still while he rigged a breast collar and a trace and tied up to the bay to drag the carcass away from the yard. The dun was small, stocky. She strained, pulling the big bay. Blue coaxed her. In the cold darkness the blood on the grass looked black, smoking. Behind the shed he let the fence down, got the dun to drag the horse through. Tim came and stood behind him, watching.

"He was long gone," Tim said.

Blue picked at the knots. The carcass would probably still stink up the house from here, but it was out of sight, outside the fence. He took everything off the dun and lifted his arms once, twice, shying her back inside the big fenced field. Then he stood looking after her, letting the rope hang down from his hand. He didn't say anything to Tim.

"It's between him and me," Tim said, in a sorry, stubborn way, low-voiced.

Blue looked at him. "Which one of them?"

In a while Tim said, "That kid, Osgood."

Blue figured he knew some of it. "I guess it was him bumped into your eye when you were out chasing nickels."

Tim looked away.

"Now we got another damn dead horse," Blue said.

Tim stared off past the dead horse into the trees. He shifted his weight. "It's between him and me," he said, sounding only stubborn this time.

It was cold and dark. Blue coiled up the rope slowly in his hand. "Okay," he said, and he walked off toward the house. Tim followed him in after a while and stood behind, watching, while he fiddled with the cold stove, getting a fire going.

After a lengthy silence, Tim said, "I never thought he'd shoot the horse." Blue didn't answer him. It wasn't his horse. He didn't know why he was filled with bitter resentment. Tim looked down at his boots. In a while, unexpectedly, he said, "I was twenty years old, or twenty-one, when you and me worked for Joe Longanecker on the Rocker S." Like he was picking up the end of something.

Blue looked at him. Then he looked away. "That was a long time ago," he said, sighing.

Tim waited again. Finally he said, in a low voice, "Did you ever think about marrying?"

Blue kept from looking around at him this time. "No," he said. "I never did." He heard the way it sounded, the stung surprise in it, and was embarrassed.

Tim ducked his head. He didn't say anything else.

Blue shut the door on the firebox. Then he walked out of the house, across the dark yard to the shed. The sky was brilliantly clear, spangled with stars. He fumbled around getting an armload of stove wood. His back was tender. He was careful how he bent over. When one of the dogs came to see what he was doing, he said irritably, "Get out of the way."

Behind the wall of the shed, something bolted off through the brush noisily. The sound of his voice had started it. In a while it would come out again, or something else would, getting at the bay horse.

After the bear was killed, while he had lain painfully in the darkness, in the rain, waiting on Tim, he had shot off his rifle once, into the black trees. He didn't know why he had done that. Before very long he had heard them again, tearing at that big bear and his dead horse, Jay. They hadn't been very close to him. He hadn't been scared. He didn't know why he had done it.

## ❂ 26 ❂

On the Fourth of July Lydia went down to Evelyn and Mike Walker's. The weather was hot and windless. She wrapped the jars of milk round with wet rags before setting them down in the hamper packed with saw chips, and wet the saw chips as well, with the clear, cold water from the Jump-Off Creek.

She had been months encountering people singly or by twos: her heart turned over when she saw there were already six men or seven standing about in the yard as she rode the mule slowly up the narrow track off the Oberfield Road. Gradually she saw among them Tim Whiteaker, Blue Odell, Mike Walker and his hired man. The others she did not know.

It was Mr. Odell who came out to meet her. He held the mule

and put a hand up for the hamper. "How are you, Mrs. Sanderson."

"Hello, Mr. Odell. This is heavy."

"I've got it."

She climbed off the mule and stiffly pulled down the skirt of her good blue dress without looking toward the several men watching her.

"I don't know if you've met all of us," Mr. Odell said gently. He was watching her as if he might be appraising her in some way.

She looked toward the others, stiffening her mouth in a deliberate smile. "No."

He pinched her elbow lightly in his hand and walked her over there. "Mrs. Sanderson," he said, gesturing vaguely. "We have a few for you to meet. This is Carroll Oberfield. He raises cattle down at the end of this road." She put her hand out and Mr. Oberfield shook it politely. He was a short man but thick-set, his hands thick from front to back and his head shaped quite round and placed solidly on the broad neck. She had it from Evelyn Walker that he was well-to-do, and that his wife lived in Maryland. They had met and married suddenly while Mr. Oberfield was on a tour East, calling on relatives. But she had been in delicate health, or of delicate constitution. She had lived with him briefly, in 1883 or '84, and not since. He spoke his wife's name occasionally. So far as anyone knew, they had never divorced.

The man who stood next to Carroll Oberfield put out his own hand abruptly. "I'm Jim Stallings, ma'am. I live over at the Goodman Station." He had a big rough face, reddish-skinned, large-featured, a smile that showed big teeth.

Beside him was an old thin bachelor, Herman Rooney. She remembered that he was the man who raised dogs. When Mr. Odell said his name, he nodded his head and took her hand lightly without shaking it. He was scrupulously clean, smelling of bath salts and shaving lotion, his mustache neatly waxed.

"You know Mike Walker, and Tim," Blue said. Neither of those two stepped up to shake her hand, they stood back and nodded. She had not seen Mr. Whiteaker since his proposal was made. She glanced toward him in stiff embarrassment. His own look was stiff too, his arm was stiff as he touched his hat.

"Do you know Otto Eckert?" That was Mike Walker's hired man. He was a bachelor, with a blond beard and pale eyes set deeply so that he seemed to peer out of the brush. He was excruciatingly shy, or he had taken a dislike of her, she could not tell which it was. She was always determinedly polite. "Hello, Mr. Eckert." He took a step backward and folded his arms up on his chest. Maybe he bobbed his head.

"Shall I bring this in the house now, ma'am?" Blue Odell lifted the hamper slightly.

"Yes. Thank you, Mr. Odell."

She followed him in, striding forthrightly while the men watched her from behind. The house was stifling hot inside. Evelyn Walker's face was scarlet and glossy.

"Oh, Mrs. Sanderson! There you are." Evelyn took hold of both her hands tightly. Her smile made a sweet bow in her wide face.

Lydia smiled, herself. "I am here," she said, sighing.

The McAnallys came last, in the late morning, sitting up on a high wagon behind a pair of brown hinny mules. They lived almost to the Umatilla-Union county line. They had left there at six-forty by Avery McAnally's watch, and come the long way without stopping except as the mules required water.

Doris McAnally was fifty, her hair coarse and black, almost without gray, her face dark and creased as muslin. Three of her children were grown and married. Two were dead. Two were half-grown: a thin, shy girl, twelve; and a boy fourteen who rode Avery's horse ahead of the wagon. Doris, when she came in the hot little house, shook Lydia's hand strongly, as if she were a man, and then kissed her once firmly on a cheek. "There," she said. "That is for getting Avery to drive us here. I haven't seen

Evelyn in a year, and we wouldn't have come now, except he must get his look at the woman homesteader."

Lydia smiled briefly, sourly. "I am famous, then."

"Well, until they have all seen you once or twice, and made up their minds that you are bound to fail!" Doris McAnally's smile was sour also. She squeezed Lydia's hand in fierce, abrupt friendship.

There was no shade at all near the house. The men carried the sawhorses and the planks down under the pine trees a hundred yards away, and the food was all brought down there by slow, hot procession. Evelyn's shy boys were carried down on Mike Walker's shoulders, but they afterward hid under the sawhorse table and would not be coaxed out.

Lydia sat down too soon: the stationman, Jim Stallings, came and took up the bench next to her, where she had hoped Doris McAnally or Evelyn Walker might sit.

Mr. Stallings was talky company. Shortly she knew he was a widower twice, with eleven children farmed out to sisters-in-law in three different states. "I've lately been considering taking off the time and going round to see them all, see if they are growing up right," he said, smiling in a slow, contrite way. "I wouldn't mind marrying again," he told her, and smiled ruefully, so it was a joke, or anyway only half serious. "But you know I'd have to take all those offspring back again if I did that, so I figure I had best stay a bachelor until they are grown. There's no hope, anyway, of finding a woman who would marry a man with eleven offspring." He looked at her sidelong, with his brows pinched up in his reddish forehead.

She smiled slowly, stiffly. "Oh I'm afraid not, Mr. Stallings, no hope at all."

He nodded. "Well I thought so," he said. "Here, Mrs. Sanderson, let's get the coffee down to our end here. I do like having the little cream to sweeten it, eh? Owing to you. I said to myself I'd got used to coffee without cream but now that I've had it again I see I was lying to myself all along." He flashed a cheerful grin.

She smiled faintly also. "I could not live long without milk," she agreed. "But I'm afraid it's sugar I miss. It is too dear for me. I have gone without for months."

"Well, sugar has gotten high right now, that's a fact. But I've heard they're going to grow it down on the Grande Ronde, and I wonder if the price of it won't come down on that account. Of course, not soon enough!"

"I don't suppose we could grow sugar beets up here."

"Oh no, ma'am, not a chance. They need those long hot summers, hot nights too. We've got but three seasons up in these mountains and that's Winter, Thaw, and August." He grinned again, enjoying what he had said. "But I guess you'd know about winters all right. It gets cold in the state of Pennsylvania, I hear."

"Yes, it's cold. But they have gotten hot long since, I imagine, and likely to stay so until October."

He smiled wider, as if he took a perverse pride in harsh weather. "Well, there's no telling here. We've had a hard frost in June and again by the end of August. Snowed once in June, I remember. There's just no telling. Soil is thin too. I don't believe it'll grow much besides tamaracks and pines and rocks."

She shook her head but she kept smiling too. She was not sure how serious he was, though the peas had not come up at all, the turnips were still small as marbles. "Oh, Mr. Stallings, I hope you're wrong. I've put so much work onto the garden."

He grinned and shook his head. "Well I shouldn't have said it. The truth is, I've never tried to grow anything myself, except once I planted a squash and the seed rotted in the ground, but I haven't got the hand for it, I know that, and you shouldn't take me for a standard. Did you put in spuds? I believe they'll grow in rocky ground well as anything only their shapes will come out crooked. They'll stand some cold too."

"They are coming up for me."

"Well good. So you see I spoke too quick. You'll be roasting spuds on the stove next winter and I'll be eating rocks, and the needles off them tamaracks."

She laughed and sipped the sweet hot coffee. As a husband, or as a father, she would surely have found him wanting, but she discovered she did not mind his company on the Fourth of July. He had an easy sociability — maybe it was the result of two wives and eleven children.

Beneath the table, one of Evelyn's boys sat on the toes of her boots, staring up under the edge of the cloth. She had not quite looked down at him. But in a while she lowered a spoon of yellow rice pudding, and when he had thought it over, he took the spoon in his own hand and licked it clean.

"Are you Junior or Charlie?" she asked him, whispering gravely.

He whispered, "Junior."

She fed him slowly, by spoonfuls, reaching below the table.

Afterward the three women walked back across the dry grass to the house, carrying up the platters and plates, and standing together in the stifling room doing up the dishes. Doris McAnally's daughter Catherine stayed in the shade under the pine trees, watching over the two Walker children, silently tempting them to play in the grass and the brush away from the benches.

Doris said in a low voice, looking out the window across the still, bright field to the trees, "Poor Catherine has got her friend already, she's not thirteen yet. I don't wonder she has turned as shy as those two little boys."

Lydia considered. Then she said, "I was twelve myself," with something like Mr. Stallings's perverse pride in bad weather.

Doris McAnally shook her head, made an unhappy clucking sound. "Well, I am over it myself, anyway, and not sorry to see it behind me."

Evelyn, in a low way, looking down at her hands wiping out bowls, told them, "I have heard if you get it early, you won't carry a baby well, but I don't know if that's true." Her eyes jumped to Lydia.

Doris shook her head again, thoughtfully. "My first girl, Muriel, was almost as early, she was thirteen, and she has two children already and never had any trouble carrying them." She looked at Lydia in her steady, unreserved manner. "Did you have that trouble, then, carrying babies?"

She liked Doris's plain straightforwardness. It made her feel steady, herself. She said, "Yes," and smiled firmly.

Doris nodded. "Do you miss having them?"

That surprised her. She looked away. "No!" Then she said slowly, stubbornly, "I am not inclined to loneliness."

"I guess I have been lonely, with five or six of my children in the same room with me," Doris said ruefully. In the moment afterward, Lydia saw the look that went between Doris and Evelyn, an understanding of something, from which she was unavoidably shut out.

Then Evelyn said suddenly, in a girlish way, impassioned, "I admire you so much, Lydia! You are brave as anyone!"

Lydia made a surprised, disbelieving sound that was not quite a laugh. But she felt better afterward. She knew there was a small, keen truth in it.

In the afternoon they lounged on the benches and on the grass in the stippled shade and listened drowsily while the men spoke of cattle prices and the progress of the depression, and the usefulness of putting up hay. Carroll Oberfield was the only one of them who had been doing it for long. He had no spring roundup to speak of. His cattle stayed all winter near the stackyards where the hay was doled out to them on the snow. Then it was a simple matter to watch over the calving, and afterward to separate out the calves for branding. Mike Walker had bought a mower and sweep himself. The hired man, Otto, was not a range hand but a skilled hayer. The two of them had just begun to cut the wild grass hay on the big field the house sat in.

While they talked about cutting and raking and shocking hay, Tim Whiteaker sat on the grass glumly and stripped the stems of weeds with his fingers. "I guess we lost as many cows to wolfers, last winter, as to starving," he said finally, but there was little quarrel in it; it had a slow, thoughtful sound.

Carroll Oberfield scrubbed the top of his round, cropped head. "Tim," he said gently, "I suppose if most of your cows were kept down on your stackyards where you could keep an eye on them, there wouldn't be too many wolfers who would bother them." He looked faintly sorrowful. "The cattle business is bound to change, Tim. There's no stopping it, you know."

Mr. Whiteaker put his chin down. Then Blue Odell began to smile slowly without looking at Tim. "He knows it, Carroll. He just doesn't like it yet."

Mr. Whiteaker shifted his place on the grass and gave Blue a ducking look and finally he smiled a little, or grimaced — it was a deepening of the long creases that framed his mouth. "You know what they say about old dogs," he said unhappily.

The McAnallys left early in the afternoon. Doris gave Evelyn and then Lydia a short, strong hug and a sorry smile and when her husband drove her off in the wagon she looked back without smiling or waving. Herman Rooney left too, and after that the spirit was gone out of the party. The men broke down the tables and benches and carried the planks up to Mike Walker's barn. Evelyn and Lydia waded in the creek with the two little boys, who were turning over rocks and undertaking to catch crawdads in a tin can. Blue Odell was the only one of the men who walked back down under the trees where they were.

"If you want company, Mrs. Sanderson, I can wait and ride you home."

"No. Thank you, Mr. Odell."

"Well all right then. We'll go on. Tim has got to be back up to the log camp tonight." He had been squatting down along the muddy bank next to their shoes. He stood up and touched his hat. "Thanks, Mrs. Walker."

"You're welcome." Evelyn stood with the edge of her skirt floating out on the water, and the palms of her hands flat on her hips, smiling in a slightly shy way.

They watched him walk away. Then Lydia began again, turning over stones in the slow, cold creek.

"You know, Mr. Odell is Indian," Evelyn said softly.

In the evening, when the air cleared and became cool, Lydia walked out for Rollin and saddled him and led him back to the house. She was the last to leave. Mike Walker carried out the hamper and stood aside awkwardly while Evelyn came for a quick, rigid embrace. When Lydia had climbed up on the saddle, he set the box in front of her. He was a big man, he reminded her in that way of Lars. But his face was strong and bony. He had a habit of looking at his wife, following her with his eyes. When he stood back from Lydia, he looked at Evelyn and seemed to wait.

Deliberately, Lydia said, "Thank you, Mr. Walker. I always enjoy our visits."

His big brows rose up into his forehead. "I do also, ma'am." He patted the shoulder of the mule.

"Good-by, Mrs. Sanderson," Evelyn said in a stout way, smiling. She had her arms folded on her bosom. Her wide face looked girlish in the sunset light.

When Rollin had taken her a short way down the road, she turned and lifted a hand to Evelyn. Evelyn held one of the little boys up in her arms. She shifted his weight onto her hip and waved slowly. She was still holding her brave smile. There had been a flag hung down from the eave of their house, in front of the south-facing window. Mike Walker was taking it down, reaching up to get it off the nails.

# ❖ 27 ❖

Jack had let Danny do pretty much all the worrying before, but now that Danny was gone he found he was doing some of it himself. He kept both himself and Harley away from Whiteaker and the Indian. They rode up the canyons north almost to the Umatilla River, looking out for rib-splayed, rheumy-eyed old cows, tick-infested calves, old rogue steers. He made sure they skinned a cow and buried the damning hide before they hauled the naked, thin-looking carcass back up to the shack. And all summer they kept to themselves, dodging whomever they happened to see without ever getting close enough for hellos.

If the kid was lonely for other company he didn't say so. He was close-mouthed anyway, probably he didn't mind their solitariness. Jack didn't think he'd discovered the knack of conversation as yet, or it might have been he didn't give a damn about it.

For himself, Jack missed having Danny there, and he went back and forth on how he felt about being so outright workless. He had had a few laid-off winters where he'd put up in town and lived on the cheap until spring, but the summer was a cowboy's working season and he'd never had one off entirely. He and Danny and the kid had spent the last one riding from Montana to Oregon, asking after jobs at every spread between, but this was the first summer he'd done nothing — just fooled away time. Sometimes dust would blow up against the sky and make him think of some cattle drive he'd been on, or a smell like burnt grass would call up a branding crew from ten years past. Then he'd be touchy for a while, restless, Harley's habits would aggravate him, he'd wish he had gone with Danny looking for work.

But other times he was happy enough with the way things were. He liked to walk the horses out in the mornings, away from the spent grass around the shack. He'd drive them slowly down off the bench to some other clearing and then sit down for a while in their long-legged shadows without any need to get back or to get anything else done. He had been a young kid when his family had come out in a wagon from Indiana. The clearest thing he remembered from it was walking out on the prairie in the evenings, through the dry, red-stemmed grass, driving the horse and the cow and the oxen slowly ahead of him and then sitting with his chin on his knees watching them feed. His family had been beaten down afterward, by bad luck and bad judgment, and when his mother died young they were all scattered, broken apart. But he didn't think of that when he was with the horses. Walking behind them down the hill under the cool trees, he thought of that kid he'd been, walking out on the prairie with the big dumb beasts.

As much as anything, what kept him and Harley at peace was the card playing. The kid was a good player, going at it thoughtfully, frowning whether he had a good hand or bad, and playing a card with slow care. He appreciated having somebody serious to play against, and Jack liked having the time to play cards whenever he felt like it. The cards they had were worn out, soft and greasy and the corners bent dog-eared, so Jack knew a lot of them by the marks and creases. But he figured the kid knew the marks too, so they were on an equal footing in that respect. They played euchre and five-card, betting with matches. Generally Jack could win two out of three at euchre — he had taught it to the kid without teaching him any of its secrets — but Harley kept even on the poker. They traded matches back and forth and neither of them ever went bust. They played outside, sitting on the grass under a tree when it was hot. When it rained they played inside on a blanket spread out on the dirt floor. It was what they mainly did. It was how Jack remembered it afterward — that summer he spent with Harley Osgood, playing for matches and waiting for neither of them knew what.

## ❄ 28 ❄

The days became long, regulated, uniform.

In the morning, the milk that had been taken the night before and let cool, must be jarred and set down in the cold cairn she had made in the piled-up rocks of the Jump-Off Creek. Then, crouching in the shadowless chill before the sun had cleared the high east ridge, she let down the goats and hung the new milk in a clean flour sack to clabber in the long day's heat, before she ate a never-varied meal of corn mush and buttermilk. She forced upon herself the habit of doing up the house immediately after breakfast as otherwise it was liable not to be done at all. Then she took the axe and the bucksaw and the black mule fitted out with a trace, and went up the Jump-Off Creek past the end of the clearing and back into the trees along the narrowing gully between the ridges. There was another, smaller creek that came down the hill and joined the Jump-Off there, and she was logging the trees slowly out from the confluence. The ground for the most part was level at that place, and the trees tended to grow straight and all of a size. Also, she had in mind to build a house in the fork of the two creeks in some coming year.

She had not much experience at cutting down trees, and not a man's arm strength, so it was slow and effortful work. With the axe she made a bird's-mouth on the down side of a tree and then sawed through slowly from the high side, stopping often to let her arms hang down tiredly, or to put an edge on the saw, or to drive in a wedge when the weight of the tree pinched the saw and hung it up. The pines grew in close. She had to carefully think out the undercut, the lean, the weight of the lopsided branching, and still she had poor luck getting a tree to fall exactly where it must, the aisles between them too narrow. When one was caught up on another, then she must go at the one holding up the first, and as often as not that one would fall wrong and she had a dangerous tangle of half-fallen timber. Then it was a slow job calculating how to get it all to come down, and a quick route to run and jump clear herself, when the critical blow was struck.

Even when a tree fell cleanly to the ground, she was only fairly started — she must go along its reach, getting the limbs sawn off one after the other, and when it was trimmed, hitch it to the mule and skid it back down the gully along the banks of the Jump-Off to the house. She did everything deliberately, carefully, there being no one else to get the work finished if she was unable — and nothing about tree falling that she had found to be out of harm's way.

Sometimes after a log was dragged in and laid up to dry, she would eat a curd of soft white cheese out of her hand, standing in the yard looking at the rack of logs. If she sat to eat a better meal in the midday, the flies would torment her, and the yellow jackets. The weather continued hot and dry. On the trail she wore by skidding the logs, dust lifted up like a scarf whenever the wind blew, and it got in her teeth and behind her eyes.

On a good day, she cut four trees.

She quit logging as soon as the sun dropped behind the high west ridge. Then she turned the mule out on the dry grass in the clearing and brought water up in pails from the creek, standing long-shadowed over the hills of potatoes while the water sank slowly into the hard reddish soil. Then the milk which she'd taken in the morning, if it was clabbered enough and drained of whey, must be pressed and the curds cut and wrapped in a clean cloth and set down in the cairn. In the cold dusk afterward, she walked out for the goats and drove them in to milk again, and set the milk out in flat pans to cool overnight.

Afterward, finally, by a candle, she ate a meal of fried corn cakes, fish or meat if she had it, or a small thin-skinned potato dug up from the edges of the garden plot. She heated water while she ate, and after eating washed out her stockings. Often, she bathed her feet and her sore hands, her itching face, in the spent and tepid water afterward. She wrote daily in the bound ledger, but gradually it became a report of unvarying weather and numbers of trees cut; she forced a small hand so the pages might not fill up before fall.

On Sundays she left off the logging. She cut and split stove wood on that day, and did up a week's clean washing, made butter, did a thorough cleaning of the house, hoed along the garden rows slowly, cutting the heads off the weeds with short, brisk strokes. On Sundays, also, in the evenings or in the cool mornings after the milk was done, she fished the Jump-Off Creek or the North Fork of the Meacham, or took the shotgun out and looked for meat. She shot hares and porcupines and rock rabbits, a few. The fishing grew poor as the summer proceeded; sometimes she propped up the pole and picked chokecherries into a tin can while watching the line. She bathed on Sunday, carrying up and heating clean water that had not, this time, seen some other use before hers.

Late in July she put down the gray mule, Bill. He had failed slowly, relentlessly, without the energy for complaint. When he gave up eating altogether, she led him a good distance from the house and put his own blanket over his head and killed him deliberately with the shotgun, only setting her mouth tight and walking off quickly afterward without looking back.

She did not see Evelyn Walker at all after the Fourth of July. A day must be taken from the logging if she went there, so it was put aside by force of circumstance — she had pledged to see the goat shed done before rounding up her steers in the fall. She wrote letters from time to time and kept them ready in case Evelyn's husband might come and take the notes back with him, as he did once in July, twice in August.

The only one she saw in a regular way was Mr. Whiteaker. On the Sunday after the Fourth of July, he came riding out of the trees at the high end of the clearing and after a moment lifted his hand stiffly. She was burying garbage in the yard. She kept on digging, only waving at him briefly, and resolutely smiling.

"Mrs. Sanderson," he said when he had come up near the hole she was digging. He stayed on his gray horse and looked down at her.

"Hello, Mr. Whiteaker."

"I'm cooking for a crew over behind Meacham," he said, in a way that was unlike him, quick and direct. "I've got a cash allowance for groceries and I would like to buy milk off you if you have it to sell."

She looked up from shoveling the garbage into its shallow hole. He ducked his chin in that characteristic way, but he kept on quickly, as if he had thought over what he meant to say. "I've been coming home on Saturday night and going back there about this time on Sunday. I would come by for it every week. I guess I would buy a gallon at a time. I would get more but I don't have any good way to haul it."

She had not got over her surprise yet. She held her hand up over her eyes, shading them from the late sun, and looked at him.

He nodded as if she had said something he agreed with. Then he said, "I brought a saddlebags, and some newspaper to set the jars in."

Then finally she nodded too, and stuck the spade down in the garbage hole. She wiped her hands on her apron and left the spade standing up there and went down to the cairn. Mr. Whiteaker brought his stiff leather sacks and followed her across the yard, letting his horse loose to crop the thin grass. He stood behind her while she lifted out four quarts.

"I guess you wouldn't want to sell any of that cheese, or the butter," he said, watching her.

Without looking around at him, she said, "I would." She set out some of it on the grass behind her.

He squatted down with his sack and packed everything in carefully. "I'll bring the empty jars back with me next time," he said. "Does that leave you short of them?"

She said, "No," though probably it would.

He nodded again and stood up and carried the sacks to his horse. When he had lifted and settled the sacks across the back of his saddle, he stood beside the horse and took a handful of coins out of his pocket and looked at her.

"Forty-five cents," she said. Without the time to figure her price carefully, she didn't know if it was too little, or too much.

He reached the money out to her, dropping it into her open hand. He mounted and started to turn the horse and then didn't.

"Meacham has got a store," he said, looking down at her. And then, unexpectedly, "If you wanted anything from there, I could bring it back for you."

She considered. Then she said, "If they have got a post office, I would be grateful if you would take down a few letters of mine to be posted."

He nodded.

She went to the house and got the several letters she had written to her mother and to her aunt. She wrapped them in a piece of newspaper tied with a string, came out again and gave him the little packet, smiling slightly. "Thank you, Mr. Whiteaker. I had thought I wouldn't have this occasion until the fall, when I must go out myself."

He sat holding her letters gingerly in one hand. The little finger was crooked, not quite lying flat along the edge of the packet of letters. Probably the bone had been broken and poorly set once. Looking at it, she felt a sudden, small, inexplicable pang.

"Well, we never get letters ourselves," he said in an indifferent fashion. It wasn't clear why he had said it. She could not think what might be expected, by way of a reply.

She said, after the little silence, "If you have time, Mr. White-aker, please come in for coffee."

He shook his head. "I'll be late getting there as it is." There was an irritable quality about it, and he touched the brim of his hat and turned the horse and rode away without saying anything else.

After that, he came every Sunday regularly to buy milk from her and to take her letters to the post office. After the first occasion he became more nearly like himself, slow to speak and diffident, but he never would come inside the house and take coffee with her. She was not sorry for that, but bothered by a dim guilt.

She sent a note with him, to have her own mail forwarded to the Meacham Station from the post office in La Grande, and finally on the second Sunday of August he brought back the letters and parcels that had been waiting.

Lydia had at one time resolved to open her mail slowly when she got it — one or two each day from earliest to last, as if she had not got them all in a bundle. But that intent was lost as soon as she saw them held out in Mr. Whiteaker's hand.

She began to smile foolishly. "Oh, Mr. Whiteaker, I am so grateful to you. How many letters are there, it looks like a lot? Please come in, I wish you would. I'll make coffee and we'll see what is in those packages. Are there two of them? You know I haven't been able to post a letter myself, from April to July, I rather worried I'd be forgotten."

He did follow her in, watching her with a slight, soft smile. "I'll get the coffee made, ma'am, if you are wanting to open those parcels."

"I do, Mr. Whiteaker. Thank you. I believe I know what is in this one from my Aunt Jessie, but not the one from my mother."

She was not able to be slow or careful, she tore the paper off the books all at once and turned them over and over in her hands. "What are they, ma'am?"

She looked up. "It's an almanac, Mr. Whiteaker, and a blank book for writing in, and Marah Ellis Ryan's book, *Told In The Hills*, which is a favorite of mine."

He smiled gently. "Well good. Is that the blank one, that has the blue cloth cover?"

"Yes."

He nodded. "It's a good color," he said.

"Yes it is." She rubbed her palm along the blank book contentedly. Then she opened the almanac and read the weather, skipping at random between January and March. "We are to have a mild winter overall, and be thawed out by March," she said.

He looked up from putting the coffee on. "Do you find you can trust that book for weather?" he said.

She laughed. "No, I never have. Have you read *Told In The Hills*, Mr. Whiteaker? I have read it three or four times, and if you haven't read it, I'll loan you it."

"No. I haven't read that one, ma'am." He ducked his chin.

"Well you ought to take it home with you then." She was unreasonably happy. She brought the other, smaller package into her lap. "Shall I open this one?"

He let his smile go out wider. "Yes, I guess you'd better."

She was more careful, folding back the paper and saving it. Inside were handkerchiefs embroidered in her mother's stitch, and within them, unexpectedly, a seed packet of purple larkspur. "Oh!" she said.

"What have you got there, Mrs. Sanderson?"

She folded out the handkerchiefs and laid the seed packet on them gently, on her lap. "They are seeds of larkspur, Mr. Whiteaker, and handkerchiefs."

He looked at her, dipping his chin again, keeping his tender, smiling look. "My grandmother always would grow larkspur," he said. "She claimed they would come up through snow."

"I know they will bloom fiercely in spite of the most bitter weather," she said. "I guess they will bloom all right in these mountains." She smiled childishly.

"I'll bet they will."

She counted her letters. There were fourteen. She didn't open them though. She held them on her lap, with the seeds of larkspur, while she drank the coffee Mr. Whiteaker had made for them both. Only after he had gone, she sat up late by a candle reading her letters slowly and rereading them. She had never had occasion to exchange a letter with her mother before this. The handwriting looked hasty, unfamiliar. She did not recognize her mother's voice in the short, sweet lines speaking of loneliness.

## ❀ 29 ❀

The summer weather stopped suddenly. There were a few days of rain and when the skies cleared it was another season entirely, the days foreshortened and cool, the wind smelling of dirt.

Tim quit the logging camp and on the next Saturday they went over to Oberfield's. Carroll had a big crew in summer and they cast a pretty wide net: generally they drove in a few steers of just about every brand that ran between the Umatilla River and the Five Points. So Oberfield had got in the habit of asking them all there in the fall, to swap steers. This year the several women made up their minds to cook a dinner meal, so it became another social occasion.

Lydia Sanderson came in the high-wheeled wagon with the Walkers, sitting up on the seat beside Mrs. Walker, holding one of the little boys on her lap. Tim let Carroll Oberfield and Blue go over there to hand the women and children down. He had not told her he would be finishing up his cooking job and she would have expected him last Sunday to come for the milk. He didn't know why he hadn't gone over there to tell her.

Carroll lifted her hamper out of the back of Walker's wagon and she followed him up to the house where Doris McAnally was already cooking. She didn't look toward Tim at all. She held one of the little boys by the hand and bent down once to listen to something he said. She had on the blue dress and a little brown cape, the neat felt hat, and she looked more womanish than was usual, holding the hand of the child. It occurred to him suddenly to wonder if she might have children of her own. He had never heard one way or the other about it.

The men spent the best part of the day standing around next to the tables, talking and smoking and waiting for the dinner to be brought on. The weather was windy and dry and bright-cold. Standing away from the shade of the buildings, in the clear mild sunlight, Tim felt a heat build up slowly under his coat and on the bare skin of his face. He stood with the other men but not listening very closely, only nodding once in a while and looking down at the ground. The larches were shedding their needles. In the wind, he heard them dropping like rain. The maples had been red for a while, but they hung on to their leaves, only letting go little handfuls when the wind gusted hard. He had given up trying to guess the weather by them, he had seen the trees surprised often enough, hunched up in full green leaf under shawls of snow.

The dinner that was finally set out was beef and hopping john, new bread sliced and spread with butter and chokecherry jam, lettuce and peas and yellow crookneck squash out of the several gardens, squash pie and berries with Mrs. Sanderson's yellow cream clabbered and poured over.

Oberfield had already let go his cook and the summer hires. He had but two hands he kept year around so they sat down to table with the neighbors, making a crowd along the benches. Tim was stuck beside one of the McAnally children, a thin girl he took to be eleven or twelve, timid and silent. She kept her elbows close in against her sides and blushed furiously pink whenever she must hand along a dish to someone. Herman Rooney took the other side of him but he kept up a steady, soft-spoken talk with Mrs. McAnally across the boards, so Tim wound up saying little. There was a kind of softness about all of the talking that went on, he thought, maybe due to the dry wind, or to the dry showering of the larch trees.

Afterward the men walked out to look at Oberfield's haystacks. They stood around in the cold sun between the stacks, passing a flask of whiskey Carroll had brought out. In June, Tim had seen an old *Sentinel*. In the financial news it was rumored that Oberfield had taken a mortgage on the five thousand acres of his that stood nearest the rail line. Tim didn't know if it was true, or if maybe he would have the money to pay it off after he shipped his steers. He might have. He looked relaxed and cheerful now, his face pink from the whiskey and the wind.

Mike Walker stood next to Tim with both his hands stuck in his jeans. He watched the flask go around. "Are you finished cooking for those loggers?" he asked.

Tim nodded. "They weren't happy. The cook they had before is still in bed with a plaster cast."

Mike looked off across the stubble field. "Were they hiring on for the logging?"

"No. I guess not. They had a full crew." He looked sideways at Mike. "You never logged, did you?"

"No." He set his mouth. "I was just thinking about it." He had about nine hundred acres, from a donation land claim and a timber claim. It was better land than they had on the Half Moon, more open and level, there was more wild grass hay on it. But he had a wife, and soon three babies, and wages he paid out in the summer when there was more work than he could do himself.

He said, "I guess Evelyn wouldn't stand for it." He flushed and smiled thinly. He was not any younger than Tim. He had closed up his house and gone down to Alicel one fall and come back in the spring with a young girl bride. He knew what he had: he held her in a kind of tender, vigilant regard.

"I guess not," Tim said, smiling with him.

The flask came around. Tim took a gingerly swallow and passed it to Blue. He thought his stomach would be all right with the food to settle it, but the whiskey burned going down. It spread heat out slowly in his chest.

Avery McAnally let the whiskey go by him, looking sheepish and unwavering all at the same time. His wife was a prohibitionist. Doris had cut out and sewn a few hundred blue ribbon temperance badges at their kitchen table over the past years. Tim had heard that one of her brothers, in a drunken craziness, had killed his wife with a pair of scissors while their six little children looked on.

"I don't know," Oberfield said in a general way. "I think things have leveled out now. Prices will come up in the spring, I expect."

Mike Walker turned his head and looked hard at Carroll as if he thought he could see in the old man's face whether it was true or not. Some of the others looked toward him too. He had started out thirty years ago with as little as any of them, and he had held on to it through the last depression, 1873. In the more than twenty years since, he had built up to twelve thousand acres and in a good year he had a summer crew that ran to eight or nine men. They gave his views a little more weight than their own.

Blue said in a soft way, not looking at Carroll, "I heard the Cattlemen's Club was thinking of getting with the Sheepmen and offering a wolf bounty again."

Tim looked at him. He hadn't heard that. Maybe Blue had got it from one of Oberfield's hands. Oberfield was the only one of them who belonged to the Cattlemen's. He nodded solemnly, shifting his weight inside his blanket coat. "We got to step forward, now that the state's pulled back. And I believe it's a sign of fair times around the corner, in as much as the money for it has got to come out of our own pockets. The vote would have gone the other way a year ago, I'm pretty sure of that, none of us could have spared the odd dollar." He said a second time, nodding, "Things have leveled out now."

Tim had kept away from Loeb's old shack since the bay horse was killed. He didn't know if the wolfers were still squatting up there or not. When Blue looked at him, he made a narrow shrugging motion and looked away.

It was cold enough so they finally trooped up to the house. The kitchen, where the women were, was hot and damp. Doris McAnally shooed them on through there into the parlor. All three of the women had their sleeves pushed past the elbows, doing up the last of the dishes. Mrs. Sanderson stood over a dishpan with her hands stuck down in the yellowish lees of the water. Her elbows were rough and reddish, she worked her arms in a short, jerky way, scrubbing.

In the parlor the men stood around or sat on Oberfield's upholstered furniture and talked about the dry weather and the fires they had had down on the Grande Ronde, and the wheat harvest around La Grande, and if there was any remedy for a spavined horse. When the women came into the parlor there was a general softening of voices, a falling off of talk. Tim gave his place to Evelyn Walker. He went across the room and stood between Blue and Avery McAnally. Lydia Sanderson had brought down her sleeves, but her narrow hands looked rough and red as her elbows. Her face was sunburnt and dry. She sat on the wide arm of the chesterfield sofa beside Mrs. Walker. Both of the little boys squirmed in there between them, burrowing back as far as they could get.

Herman Rooney had brought his accordion and he played "The Dying Californian," "Brennan on the Moor," "Green Grow the

Rushes-O." Mrs. Walker had a sweet clear voice and she knew every word. With her eyes fixed on the floor somewhere in the center of the room, she sang out loud, without any of her usual girlish shyness. Blue knew those songs pretty well too, and he sang along with her in a loud steady voice, so that the other men began to come in when they knew a chorus or as they remembered words.

Tim couldn't make out Lydia Sanderson's voice among the others but she looked down at her clasped hands and mouthed the songs gravely. He only knew the chorus of "Brennan on the Moor" himself. The third time it came around he got the words out meekly, looking down at his boots.

No one stayed late. The McAnallys left in the early afternoon, the boy riding Avery's horse and driving the two steers they had got from Carroll's gather. Doris McAnally stayed turned on the seat to regard the other women silently until the wagon took her on out of view. Once the McAnallys had gone, the gathering took on a damp quality, faintly mournful. Tim wasn't sorry when the rest of them began to break off abruptly. He and Blue went out to catch up the gray mare and the dun. Mike came up behind them while they were saddling the horses.

"You ought to ride back with us as far as the creek," he said, standing with his hands pushed into his pockets. "We'll be going along the same way."

Blue looked over at Tim. "I guess we could stand the company," he said.

Tim ducked his chin. "All right."

They helped Mike hitch up his wagon. Mrs. Walker came out of the Oberfield house while they were doing it. She carried one of the little boys up on her hip, his sweaty head slumped against her bosom. "Mike," she said. "Would you lift him into the back. He's gone off asleep."

Mike took the child gently from her, lifted him over the side-board, set him down on a folded-up quilt. He pulled out the edge of the quilt and put it over the boy and patted him lightly on the shoulder.

"Junior is sleeping too, and he's getting about too heavy for me to carry," Mrs. Walker said, watching her husband.

"Well, I'd better go in and get him myself then." He patted her on the hand in the way he had done the child and went up to the house. Tim stood back faintly embarrassed, as if he had been watching them secretly.

Evelyn Walker hugged her own arms. She'd not put a coat on, and the wind kept on cold. She considered Tim and Blue in a half-shy way. "Will you keep Mike company, then?" she said. She was a big, heavy girl, but Tim thought her wide face was pretty, the skin smooth, fine-complected.

"I guess we'll ride along some of the way," Blue said.

Mike came out with the boy and laid him down next to the younger one, huddled up under the quilt. "What else have you got for me to carry?" he said to his wife.

"There's nothing as heavy as that," she said, and went back toward the house. The wind blew her skirt out sideways.

In a minute, Carroll Oberfield came out ahead of the two women. He toted Mrs. Sanderson's hamper and an empty wicker creel that might have brought lettuces or peas. Mrs. Sanderson followed him out, carrying a pie tin flat in front of her, bundled up in newspaper. An uneaten pie, maybe. Blue let down the tailgate and Carroll put the hamper and the creel along the sideboard. Mrs. Sanderson kept hold of the pie.

By then Mrs. Walker had come out. Mike looked at her. "Well, Mother, are you ready to start home?"

She slid a girlish, fond look at him. "I guess I am."

Tim thought Mrs. Sanderson might offer her hand to Carroll but she didn't. Only after she had climbed up in the wagon and Mike's wife up to the high seat, she said in her usual serious way, inclining her head over the side of the wagon, "It was kind of you to have us all, Mr. Oberfield."

He nodded, seeming serious too. "Enjoyed your company, ma'am."

Oberfield stood there on the porch as Evelyn Walker drove the wagon off and it was Mrs. Sanderson who lifted her hand once and got a wave from him.

"Thanks, Carroll," Blue said, and stuck out his hand to shake. Tim shook the old man's hand too, and Mike did. Then they rode their horses over and got their steers and Mike's and two that were CrossTie-branded, and drove them slowly down the road after the wagon.

It wasn't much of a road, the ruts were cut deep and hardened. Tim could see Mike's wife keeping the wheels up on the shoulder where she could, but the ride generally was rough. Mrs. Sanderson sat in the back, behind the high seat, holding the boys' heads on her stretched-out lap after the first hard bump had woke them crying. Tim couldn't hear if the two women were talking at all. Sometimes Mrs. Walker would turn around and she and Mrs. Sanderson would pass a soft look or a tired one between them, and she would run her eyes over the two boys and then swing around again.

The sun fell behind the mountains, casting up a red stain that dimmed gradually to purple. The wind dropped off, but the darkness was sharp with cold. Tim buttoned his coat up and blew on his hands. By the moon there was enough light to see the road, but he got so he couldn't make out Mrs. Sanderson's narrow sunburnt face, just the solid shadow of her there, braced against the jounce of the wagon. He had begun to think of saying something to her about his not coming after the milk, but he didn't know how he ought to bring it up, or if he would get the chance.

Evelyn Walker pulled the wagon over, where Chimney Creek ran in a slippery sheet across the road. Tim heard Mike say gently, "Here is Chimney Creek, boys," as if they might not know it. There was a trail that ran back along it to their place. It was the springs of the Chimney that they had dammed up into a pond.

They sorted out the steers there in the road, in the cold moonlight. There were five Half Moon steers, four that were Mike's and the two CrossTie.

In the darkness, Tim got up a little courage. He rode over to the wagon. "I don't know if Mike was planning to see you and those steers home in the dark," he said to Mrs. Sanderson. "If he was, we could as well do it ourselves. It's not out of the way."

It was Mike who answered, pulling up his shoulders and glancing at his wife. He said, "I guess she's going to stay over and go home in the morning." He didn't say anything about the milch goats. Maybe she had brought them along to his place and left them in his barn all day.

She said, "Thank you, Mr. Whiteaker," in a tired voice, or keeping her voice low for the sake of the sleeping boys. After the one occasion, when he had brought her packages up from the post office, she had become, again, gently solemn, firmly polite.

Tim ducked his chin. He took a breath. "When I finished that work for the log camp, I meant to get over to the Jump-Off to let you know about it. But we got busy and I didn't make it."

There was a short silence. Then she said, as if it was an answer, "I don't believe I ever thanked you, Mr. Whiteaker, for bringing that milk trade to me."

He thought about what he ought to say. "I guess we both got the benefit of it," he said after a moment.

He saw her nodding. "Yes."

Blue touched his hat, began to move his horse away. "We'll be seeing you," he said.

Tim glanced toward him, but couldn't see his look in the darkness. He touched his own hat and followed Blue and the steers up the steep rise of the trail. He heard Mike starting his and Mrs. Sanderson's steers, and the wheels of the wagon making a crackly noise on the cold, rocky ground. The horses grunted, scrabbling up on the frosty mud. At the top of the ridge Blue let the dun stand a minute, letting the steers go on down the trail. When Tim came up alongside him, he never said anything to him. They both looked back after the wagon but it was gone by then. They couldn't hear anything but the horses breathing and the creek falling downhill in the cold darkness.

# ❋ 30 ❋

The clearing along the Jump-Off Creek was unfenced, and the grass was patchy, eaten down over the summer by the mule and the two goats. Evelyn Walker's husband let Lydia bring her steers down onto the Owl Meadow along the northeast of his property. There was an old fence there and the wreck of a cabin. He and Otto Eckert hadn't mowed the field, they hadn't been able to get the mower up there over the poor trail. So she patched the low places in the fence, wiring up the old pine poles, and in twenty days, riding the mule purposefully up every draw and gully, scouting the open timber and the burnt clearings and the shoulders of the ridges, she slowly brought fifteen steers down onto the meadow. She found them singly or in pairs — once a bunch of five that had come to a salt lick she had not known about, on the edge of Tim Whiteaker's property.

The mule was steady as he ever had been, dependable and tireless, and she knew enough to stay back from a steer, to come up to it gently and let it go ahead of her at its own slow gait. But if one took off unexpectedly, the mule would not jump quick to head it. While it bolted away startled into the brush, he was apt to flatten his ears and keep on at an unvarying jog-trot while she flailed his rump in a rage. It was wearying work and little reward in it. Her back ached from the long riding. She wished, for the first time in her life, for a willing and quick horse.

But she liked the methodicalness, at least — maybe even the forced unhurriedness. There was no rain. The frost had brought up a glossy gold in the aspens and the brush willows. The maples were naked, their leaves filling up the gullies with a dry yellow duff that lifted and rattled softly when the wind blew. The timber felt open, light. There was a certain pleasure in riding out every day in the silent company of the mule, crossing the long, golden ridges slowly in a bright wind.

There was a spring that made a reddish bog in a low corner of the Owl Meadow but no clear water in it. She had to bring water half a mile from another spring, hauling it in pails. By the time there were fifteen steers on the meadow, she was going down and back for the water six times a day, or seven. It was the worst of the work. There was a saucer formed among the stones of the old chimney where the cabin had fallen down, and she let the pails of water into it. But it leaked out slowly onto the ground, and often when she came onto the meadow in the afternoon the steers would be standing muddy-legged around the empty basin of the chimney, or snuffling the mud of the spring.

On one of the last days, a steer was stuck up to its belly in the quickmud in that bog. From half a mile off, coming in tiredly after a second gainless day, she heard it lowing dully and steadily with an unpitiful sound of complaint. She rode to the edge of the drying-up pond and looked at the steer unhappily. She was loath to get out in the mud herself. But the stupid steer kept up its crying, and made no effort to get clear of the bog on its own. Its eyes were glazed, blank.

She stood down beside the mule and dispiritedly bunched her skirt, pulling it up under the belt so her long shins in black stockings were bared above the boot tops. She stepped her boots unwillingly into the sucking mud and pitched a noose of rope around the steer's big horns. He kept up his steady complaining. She backed out of the mud and tied off the rope to the saddle horn of the mule, backed him up slowly until it was taut. The mule squatted back hard until the saddle tried to stand up on its pommel, but the big steer stood sullenly in the wallow, eyes bulging, neck twisted over by the pull on its horns. Lydia put all her own weight on the rope too, planting her feet and yelling at the mule, but the steer stood where it was. Finally she went into the trees and got a stick. She slogged out into the mud again and hit the steer hard across the nose. It bellowed in surprise and eyed her, white-edged. She yelled at the mule and the rope twanged tight a couple of times, but by then the steer's eyes had glazed again and it stood glumly in the mud, unmoving.

"Damn you!" Lydia said suddenly, harsh and loud.

She hit the steer's head again, swinging the long stick in flat and hard between the eyes, a cracking blow. The steer rocked once, silently — for a wild moment she thought she might have killed it — then it lurched ahead suddenly in the mud, bellowing and slinging its horns, hurling mud and slobber in a short, spattering flurry.

Lydia staggered quick out of the mud herself, grabbing along the rope for Rollin. She flung a leg up over the mule's back and held on to the saddle, hanging half off it while the mule sprang out of the way of the steer's short, mad lunge. The mule had never been inclined to buck, but the rope pulled around under his tail when the steer staggered past him, and he snorted wildly, put his head down and bucked up his back. She would have stayed on him if she'd had both stirrups, a solid seat. But she was hanging off the saddle clumsily and his one stiff-legged bounce shook her off. She hit on her back and got up quick, scrabbling around to watch the steer. He kept bellowing and hooking his horns, trying to get loose of the rope, but he stood in one place, cross-legged and swaying, as if he hadn't figured out yet that he was unstuck from the mud.

Lydia got shakily on the mule again, setting her boots well in the stirrups. Then she sidled up along the steer's shoulder. Rollin was set stubbornly on keeping away from the slung horns, she had to pull his head up hard, twisting the reins, kicking him, to get him in close enough, and then she leaned out, grabbing warily for the rope. She tried five or six times, reaching in and out, before she got the rope loose of the steer.

By then her mouth was aching and full of blood — she had bit her cheek, jarred her teeth, when Rollin had bucked her off. She sat on the mule, rocking and keening a little, and feeling the inside of her mouth gingerly with her fingers, while she watched the steer staggering off irritably across the grass. She had a piteous impulse to go home. She would have liked to leave the big dumb steers standing around the chimney basin and ride Rollin away now, with her handkerchief inside her mouth stopping the blood. She did put the handkerchief in her mouth. But then she got the pails and walked slowly, bitterly, down to the other spring. After a while she walked with the bloody handkerchief wadded up in the pocket of her sweater, but the taste of blood stayed in her mouth, and a sourness, from that moment standing scared and frozen facing the mad steer.

Evelyn Walker was sitting on the dry leaves at the edge of the Owl Meadow, with the two boys climbing on her, when Lydia walked up the long timbered hill the fourth time, lugging water.

"I have brought you a lunch," Evelyn shouted to her. She held up a sugar sack.

Lydia let out the water into the chimney and came to where Evelyn sat, in the striped shadow under the maple trees. Her mouth was stiff but she smiled and deliberately kept from telling about it. "Evelyn, I hope you didn't walk up from your house that long way."

Evelyn's face looked pink and happy. She had spread a cloth on the leaves and she brought sandwiches out of her sack, and radishes, milk in a mason jar, and a chocolate cake wrapped up in a clean towel. "We had a good ride, don't worry. We drove the wagon as far as we could get and then we unhitched and all three of us rode Judy up the hill without a saddle and we've only been waiting a little while for you." She gestured, and then Lydia saw her placid white mare browsing with the cattle.

"Well I am quite filthy for picnicking," she said, sighing. At the spring she had rinsed out her sore mouth, washed mud and blood from her hands, but the dress was spattered with mud and the steer's yellow slobber, her skin and clothes smelled of cattle and sour fear-smell.

Evelyn said solemnly, positively, "Well you are cowboying, and liable to be dirty because of it." The boys stood coyly behind her, peering at Lydia across their mother's shoulders.

Lydia rubbed the sore palms of her hands on the front of her skirt and smiled gingerly, with her sore mouth. She had not thought of herself, before now, as cowboying. "The truth is, I am half starved," she said. She sat down stiffly on the ground and when Evelyn handed over one of the sandwiches she ate slowly, chewing on the side of her mouth that was not raw.

"I believe I must have about all of them," she said tiredly, watching the steers crowding up to the water. "I have not seen any but cows and calves since yesterday morning."

"Fifteen," Evelyn said. She put a sound of assurance in it, as if she'd named a grand number.

"I think I'd be advised to let back six of them," Lydia said ruefully. "They're last year's calves I think. You can see they're small yet. I would get more for them at three years old when they've put on their full weight." She had got this from Evelyn's husband when he had ridden up to the Owl Meadow with her, behind the two steers from Carroll Oberfield's. On that occasion he had shown her a little of driving cattle, riding along one side of them and then on the other to keep them headed right, and he had managed to tell her half a dozen useful things about the ranching business without bringing up her inexperience at all.

"If there are nine, I won't be discouraged," she said firmly. "That's enough to see me another year without starvation. Only I suppose I shall be on bad terms with ground corn before then." She smiled grimly.

Evelyn had Charlie in her lap now. She smiled, but slow and irresolute, while pressing her cheek against the crown of Charlie's head. She might not have known what response was called for. Then she said, "Claud Angell never had many cattle, I guess," as if it were a reassurance.

They passed the milk back and forth. It was tepid, thick. It left a yellow skin inside the emptied mason jar. They broke the chocolate cake also, and fed pieces of it silently to the two little boys. Lydia licked her long fingers. "Oh, I have an awful love of sweets."

"You are so thin," Evelyn said, shaking her head, smiling as if she were shy.

Lydia looked down at her hands and turned them, looking at the lean wrists. "I used to stand in my shift, sideways to the mirror, and press my arms to my sides. My arms were thin as sticks, and still are, but when the fleshy part was flattened I thought they looked decently rounded." She smiled, belittling that girl she had been.

Evelyn began to redden. "I used to wish I had some thin, but Mike likes plumpness, I guess, so I had better keep what I have now."

Riding up to the Owl Meadow, Mike Walker had behaved in a thoughtful way, faintly sympathetic, as if he had made up his mind finally that she was not a man who was scared, but a woman who wasn't. Lydia had got to like him rather better since then. She said, keeping her smile, "He loves his Evelyn, I believe."

Evelyn hid her pleased look behind Charlie, who was climbing out of her lap and onto Junior's back as he lay on the grass watching bugs.

After a while Lydia said, thinking of it slowly, "My mother said I would put on weight when I was full grown, but I never did.

She is well filled-out herself. I look like my dad, I guess. He always was thin, even before he was sick. His mother, my grandmother Bennett, was thin too."

Evelyn seemed to consider; Lydia saw a solemn look come in her face. "I take after my mother," she said slowly. Then she said in a low voice, "I am going down there after Mike takes the cattle out. He is taking me and the boys to Alicel and leaving us until the spring." She looked at Lydia. "Mike always has taken me down there to have my babies, there being no woman nearby here if I had a trouble." Her face began to redden again. "I told Mike he could get you to stand by me now, but he was already set on leaving me at my mother's."

Lydia pulled her shoulders in a little and kept a stiff smile. "Shall I not see you then, until spring?"

"Oh! I hope you'll go down with us as far as Summerville anyway. You said you would ride out in the fall for your groceries, we can go that far in each other's company, can't we?" She gave Lydia a shy sideward look. "Will you miss me very much? I do hate leaving."

Lydia didn't know what she ought to answer. She looked out at the cattle fixedly, without noticing them at all. "I have never been inclined to loneliness," she said finally, but it had a sound in it that embarrassed her — something like a child's balkiness.

She had never attended a birth, only her own fruitless miscarriages — and the truth was, she had had a vivid dread of being summoned for Evelyn's confinement. She didn't know where the quick, small grief came from now. It was unexpected, inexplicable.

# ❊ 31 ❊

*20 Sept* Went down to Summerville on the 18TH leaving the goats w Mr Whiteaker & Mr Odell and riding down w Walkers. The weather has held dry and in the Valley the air was heavy & warm, the colors of things dull & sooty. Mrs Bird at whose house I stayed a night last Spring received me offhandedly w/o surprise or curiosity, so I straightaway lost any little self-satisfaction brought down from the Jump-Off Creek. Mr Walker had sold my few cattle w his own when he went out to La Grande on Sat last, and got as good a price as might be, but when I had shoed the Mule and bought Groceries I found I could not afford to shoe myself and went directly back up the Ruckel Rd, was glad enough to see the poor little House again, as Town tired and discouraged me. I shall not see Evelyn Walker now nor any other woman until the Spring, and must harden my heart not to be Lonely. I did cry a little to see her go, and she cried hard. The little boys shed tears too, for the only reason that their Mother cried! Rose will freshen before long I think and I have promised the Kid to them if it is born healthy and still alive in the Spring. O I did spend a little money w/o thought of usefulness, bought a baker's dozen of jonquil and plan to plant them w the Larkspur, as those colors will be bright together and say Farewell to Winter!

# ❀ 32 ❀

They loaded the thirty steers at the Goodman Station and rode in the smoking car down to La Grande. They had used to drive the cattle down on horseback, but it was more trouble than it was worth trying to keep a bunch of half-wild steers together on the shoulder of the overland road with those eight-mule freight wagons going past them in both directions in a steady traffic and the steers shedding a pound each, for every jittery mile. It was cheaper, they figured, to leave the horses and the dogs with Jim Stallings at the station and ride the train down.

The UP rail line followed the rise of Meacham Creek from just west of its junction with the Umatilla River up to the Kamela Station on the old Oregon Trail, maybe forty miles of slow climb through the north end of the Blue Mountains and five stops between on the long grade. After that the rails ran downhill to La Grande, snaking along the Railroad Canyon from the summit. When they had passed Kamela, the trees began to thin, standing together in sparse bunches with brown grass matted between, and at intervals they began to see the stubble of a few marginal wheat fields, and cattle standing idly inside wire fences. Finally there was a place where the train came out onto a treeless bluff and below them the city was spread out straddling the rail line. Smoke rose up from it, brown, seeping into the gray underbelly of the clouds.

Tim scraped a little clean place on the window glass and looked out. He was wound-up. He still tended to feel anxious when he got among so many people. It was something he should have gotten over by now, it was something a kid would feel and he hadn't felt like a kid in a long time. But there it was. He looked out the window and shifted his seat slightly and rubbed the armrest with his thumb. He didn't know if Blue got unsettled at all, coming down to town — he hadn't ever brought it up with him. Alongside of him, Blue smoked a cigarette, holding it with three fingers and sitting back inside the crown of smoke.

They were left off at the station ahead of the steers, and had to stand around waiting by the squeeze chutes and the pens, holding their shipping papers, until the cattle cars were put on the siding. There was another wait after that until the railroad cowboys got around to unloading the cars and writing down a corral number on their papers. Then they went to find a buyer they knew.

The streets in the workingman's district were muddy, lined with seedy huts and warehouses and freight docks where the mules stood wet-necked and the warehousemen loaded the long wagons or tied the loads down or stood in the mud together smoking and talking. Sweeney had a barn and a jumble of pens at the dead end of one of the streets. He was tallying sheep at a squeeze gate. They stood and waited until the last woolly went through and he had written the number in his book. Then he looked around at both of them.

"Whiteaker," he said, after he had thought about it. "And Odell." Sometimes he wouldn't remember their names from one time to the next. But he had always dealt with them in a fair way. They hadn't gone to anybody else for four or five years. He stuck his hand out now and they each shook it.

"We've got thirty steers if you're buying any," Blue said.

"Sure. Sure. I'm always buying. I could get over there and have a look at them in a couple of hours and if you come by here in the morning I'll have a price for you. That be all right?"

Tim ducked his chin. "How are prices holding up?" he said. "Are they getting any better?"

Sweeney was a redhead with bright blue eyes and colorless lashes. He looked at them unblinking. "Well you know prices are low, but they haven't gone down in a while. I believe maybe things have leveled out. They've been getting twenty-five, twenty-six cents for wheat. That's up a little from what it was. But you heard about the fires we had. Burned up a few thousands acres of wheat and rangeland I guess." He shrugged up his shoulders. "That might be why the price is gone a little higher. That's always the way it works, sad to say. I heard you had a dry summer up there too."

"It was dry."

Sweeney nodded. He looked over at the sheep and then back at them. "You got a pen number for me?"

"One-eight," Blue read off the papers.

Sweeney nodded again and wrote it down in his book. "Well, okey-dokey," he said. "You come over tomorrow and we'll settle up. I think we can come to fair terms."

They shook his hand again and went back down the street. It began to rain a little, pocking the wooden walks. When they used to drive the steers down, they'd put the horses up at a livery, leave the dogs tied in a stall they paid a horse price for. Now they only had themselves to put up. They carried their kit bags through the rain, along the wet wood walk to the Bullshead, which was a saloon that rented beds in an upstairs loft and sometimes on a pay night sold space on the floor between the beds. There was a cleaner place nearer the railyards but the man who owned it had seen something or been part of something in the Klamath Indian Wars and he wouldn't rent a bed to Blue.

When they had paid for the beds, they stood together at the Bullshead bar, drinking beer the color of cat's eyes. Tim leaned on his elbows to take the weight off his bad knee. The long time sitting in the train had made it stiff.

"I need to eat something," he said, without looking at Blue. The beer was cold. It made a cold puddle in his belly. He had

used to drink all night without bad effects. But he had gradually
gotten so he couldn't drink on an empty stomach without feeling
sick right away. For a long time now, coming down to La Grande
in the fall, he had been getting drunk out of habit and without
taking any satisfaction from it.

"Don't puke it up later," Blue said, letting out his slow, soft
grin.

Tim went alone down the street to a cafe and sat on a stool at
the counter. He set his kit bag down under his feet. There wasn't
anyplace to leave it at the Bullshead without having it walk off,
so he had to pack it around with him. He ate eggs and a pork
chop and bread, and washed it down with coffee. The cook had
a heavy hand with the bread but it had been a while since he had
eaten eggs or a pork chop, and the coffee was good, strong and
fresh. He wished for something sweet afterward, but from where
he sat at the counter he could see the chocolate cake sitting on
a plate in the kitchen, and the flies crawling over it, so he paid
and went out without trying any.

It had stopped raining but it was near dark by now and the
low sky looked blue-black, the color of a new gun. The air didn't
smell like rain, all he could smell was the refuse in the runnels
along the curbing, and coal smoke, and a fish and grease smell
from the cafe. The street in front of him went away straight until
it arrowed to a point and disappeared. He looked down it. The
foothills lumped up brown behind the arrow point and behind
them the bluish mountains were cut off under the low sky.

The Bullshead was crowded and noisy and Blue had gone from
there. Tim went to the bar and drank a single beer slowly. He
figured he knew where Blue was, there was a whore he liked to
go to over in the Old Town. In the wild railhead towns, when
they had been pretty young, they had used to walk along in front
of the cribs, he and Blue, walking stiff as roosters, looking sideways
at the whores standing in their shawls in the open doorways.
Sometimes they had even turned and walked back along the row

of doors eyeing the women a second time until they'd picked two who suited. That seemed like a hell of a long time ago. The woman Tim had lately gone with had a house on an alley behind a produce seller. The cowboy who had showed him the house the first time had said he didn't know if she made her living whoring or if she had other work besides. She had clean brown hair, a placid face, and so he had gone back there when he was in town, and when he had a little money. Blue had been seeing the same whore once or twice a year for five or six years. One of her children was dark-skinned, had a wide slow smile.

Tim drank the beer and then took his kit bag and went out. He didn't have anything in mind. He just walked. They had brought electric lights into the city two or three years before. There were street lights on Adams Avenue. He walked down that street until the walks and the lights gave out and then walked back in on Washington. Eventually, without deciding to, he went over into the alley where the woman's house was. It was little and shabby. When he saw it he remembered her name was Margaret or Madeleine. He went up slowly onto the narrow porch and rapped against the door. His belly felt a little sour, from the beer.

The woman who answered the door had a face he did not know. He stood there dumbly, holding his kit bag with both hands. After a moment, she smiled slightly, questioning, and said, "Oh I guess you are looking for Madeleine."

"Yes."

"She has gotten married you know."

He stood again silently, embarrassed. The woman kept smiling in that uncertain way. "You can come in if you want, though."

She had yellowish skin, but her hair was clean, a good honey color, and she didn't otherwise look sick. She smiled and talked to him a little, sitting on the edge of the bed, and then stopped talking when she saw he had little to say. She took off her dress and a soiled little shift and lay on the bed with her legs open, waiting for him. She kept smiling, but she watched him in a cautious way, because of his silence. She wasn't fat, but now he could see her belly looked swollen, as if she was pregnant, or tumorous. If he had seen it sooner, he might not have used her. But he couldn't keep himself from her now she was lying open and naked in front of him. He lay down on her gently, and then urgently, and afterward dressed and got his kit bag, put a dollar on her nightstand, and went out of her house onto the dark street where it had begun again to rain.

Blue was standing at the bar in the Bullshead. He had struck up some talk with the thin young kid standing next to him. Tim stood on his other side and drank a beer. He drank it slowly, running his fingers up and down in the dampness on the outside of the glass. He half listened to Blue and the kid. They talked about horses, and about outfits that were going broke, and the kid told a story about a big bull that split open every cow he covered. Tim had heard the story three or four times before, told better, and the kid didn't know a damn thing about horses. He quit listening.

"You're not saying much," Blue said. The kid had gone off. Tim looked after him.

"I guess I'm getting too old," he said.

Blue shrugged his shoulders, smiling. "A kid like that doesn't even know enough to put his boots on before his spurs."

Tim laughed. "I guess you were never that green."

Blue shook his head, smiling wider. "No I never was."

They drank one more beer and then Tim said, "I believe I'll go upstairs."

Blue looked at him. "You sick?"

"No. I guess I'm tired out."

He climbed the stairs to the beds they had rented. He put his kit under a bed and sat on the edge of the thin mattress and looked around in the darkness at the other cots. The low ceiling sloped lower to join the wall behind him. He'd have to watch his head, getting out of bed. The attic smelled of sweat and foul breath and urine. He lay down on the bed without taking his boots off. In a little while he began to smell the stale sex on himself. He stood again and left his damn kit bag where it was and went down the narrow stairs. When he didn't see Blue there, he went through the crowd and outside onto the porch. He stood with the noise and the lighted windows at his back and sucked the damp air.

"You the guy with that Indian?"

It was the thin kid who had stood talking to Blue. His face was pink.

"Yes."

The kid gestured with his head. "Seen him getting beat up in the alley behind here. You know where I mean?" He looked away, embarrassed.

Tim went down the wet planks and around the corner into the mud. There was an alley alongside the saddlery and he turned up it, going past the trash bins and an outside stair. At the back, where the outhouses stank in a row between the buildings, there were three men hitting each other.

"Hey," he said, and all of them turned toward him. Blue, once he had had seen it was Tim, looked back at the other two, who stood huffing and watching Tim, letting their hands hang down. One of them spat once — maybe it was blood. Blue looked hunched. Tim heard him wheezing a little.

"It's an Indian," one of them said to Tim. He shifted his weight, smiling enough so Tim could see the white edge of his teeth in the darkness.

"Not much of one," Tim said. Blue laughed, or anyway made a sound that was like a laugh, short and low. He didn't have that much Indian in him, a Salish grandmother married in a church to a Catholic Englishman. He looked more Indian than he was. He looked like his grandmother, maybe.

The two men watched Tim. "I know him," Tim said. "He's just a poor old cowboy." He lifted his hands, making a gesture like he was sorry.

The one who had smiled, smiled again. He looked sidelong at Blue. "He looks Indian," he said.

Tim lifted his hands again. "Yeah, he does." Then he said, "He was raised up by wolves, though. I guess there's no way of telling what breed he is for sure."

Blue laughed again. Tim began to smile himself. It had been a while since he had made that joke.

The other two looked from Tim to Blue. After a while Blue made a gentle movement, maybe he was walking off, but the smiling man put out a hand, catching him by the elbow. Blue made a slight hissing sound and threw off the hand and the man grunted, surprised, and swung his hand up in a fist that hit Blue on the ear. Tim jumped for the other one, the big one who had spit. He grabbed hold of him by the lapels of his coat and hit the big reddish face. That was the only good blow he got. Something struck him on the forearm, it felt like a piece of metal, and his fingers, his whole arm, went numb, prickling, and then blossoming with pain. He hit with his other hand, his good hand, clumsily, and then he got hold of the coat again and wrestled until they tripped and fell rolling in the stinking mud under the stair risers. The man's breath whistled shrill next to his ear. Mud was in his teeth, he wanted to spit it out but he couldn't get the air to do it, the man had got around on top of him, pushing his big chest down over his face. The smell of the man's sour sweat and breath gagged him. The man hit him three or four times in the side, short soft blows, no leverage, then brought his knee up suddenly between Tim's legs. Tim's stomach came up.

"Ah, Jesus," the man said, rolling off him.

Tim rolled over too, spitting to clear his mouth of mud and the bitter vomit.

"Ah, Jesus," the man said again, and stood up, scrubbing his chin and his shirt front with his hands.

Tim lay where he was, drawn up protectively around his genitals. His ears rang. He breathed carefully through his mouth. After a long time he heard a Pianola playing through the wall of the building next to him, and after that Blue said, "Shit," on a high laughing gasp. Tim made a small sound too, meaning it to be a laugh, but it came out soft, a sigh.

In October the weather for the most part stayed clear and windy. It was very cold at night, and whenever the wind fell away, the grass in the mornings was frozen hard, painted white with rime. She had no instinct yet for the weather in this country, and when it clouded over she looked for snow. But under the low overcast the air warmed and only a little rain fell, making no sound at all, puddling in the dead brown prints her boots had tracked on the frozen grass.

In the thin drizzly daylight she squatted under the sloping roof of the shed, out of the rain, and let the goats down. She didn't see Mr. Odell until his horse blew air and signaled her. He had by then come most of the way up the long clearing toward the house. He sat on his horse in an odd way, arms held down stiffly, and in a moment she made out the big bundle he was holding up on his lap. It was a moment more before she saw a dog's legs dangling below a blanket edge.

She went over to him without a word. He gave her an apologetic look, no part of his wide smile. "He's dying, I guess, but I brought him over here in case there was something you knew to do for him."

She reached up for the dog, and Mr. Odell gave the weight over gently to her. The dog's body inside the blanket was slack, cumbersome. She held him up against her chest and carried him into the house, put him down on the floor on the braided rug. Mr. Odell had followed her in. He stood next to the door, looking at the dog.

"I imagine he got hold of a strychnine bait," he said in a low way. When she looked back toward him he said, "Tim's out looking for Hangdog. We figure they both got hold of it. Hangdog always would eat anything and Tag was more particular. If Tag only took a lick off it, he'd have had time to walk home before it started to kill him." He said it flatly, without tenderness, but he kept his voice low as if he meant not to wake the poor dog.

She had not seen how strychnine killed an animal, only the bodies of the long-dead ravens and the fox kit on the trail beside Buck's Creek. She looked at the yellow dog. He breathed shallowly with his mouth unshut, his swollen tongue pushing against his teeth. There was bloody slobber and vomit crusted on his muzzle, bloody feces soiling his haunches and his tail.

"I don't know what to do for him, Mr. Odell. I don't have any experience with strychnine."

He nodded. "Well I didn't expect you would. But I thought I'd ask about it." He made a small motion toward the dog, an incomplete gesture, and then kept standing there.

"We can see if he will take a little warm water," she said, because he seemed to expect her to take some action. "Or at least bathe his gums with a blackberry tea. Maybe he is over the worst now and if he is kept warm and left to rest, he'll take a favorable turn."

The man did a short sidestep, rustling inside his damp coat. "I guess that's not too likely," he said, without looking toward her.

She did not answer.

He kept looking at the dog with no particular feeling in his face. "Well then if you don't mind, I'll let him stay where he is until there's a change."

"Yes." She stood and put water to heat and broke a few dry blackberry leaves in a bowl.

"I'd better turn out that horse," Mr. Odell said, and went outside. He was gone quite a while. She rubbed the dog's gums and poured a little of the tea behind his teeth, sitting down on the rug with his bony head in her lap. After a while Mr. Odell came in again. He had her two pails in his hands.

"I figured it couldn't be too far off from how a cow gets done," he said. "So I went ahead and finished those goats." He let out his wide mouth somewhat without fully smiling. It made her think suddenly of his face, the constrained look he had kept all the while she had sewed up his bloody back.

"Thank you, Mr. Odell."

He put down the pails and rubbed his palms along his pants. "I'll sit down with the dog if you'll show me what to do."

He sat as she had been, holding the dog's head, and from time to time dribbling a little tea down the back of the swollen throat. She gave him a wrung out wet rag and he daubed at the crusty nostrils and under the filthy tail. In the tiny room Lydia stepped over the man's legs repeatedly and over the body of the dog. She did it in an offhand way, not apologizing, so that after a couple of times he quit apologizing himself, maybe understanding he was an obstacle of no great matter to her.

When the milk was put up, she made a corn mush breakfast enough for both of them without asking if he had eaten, and he accepted it without a false show. The smell of the dog in the close room was rank, sour, but neither of them referred to it. They ate in silence, listening to the dog's terrible wheeze, and the rain dribbling off the eaves of the roof. Afterward she sat on the camelback trunk, using the time as well as she could to finish the edge of a piece of flour sacking. The man watched her openly, as if he would learn the stitches from following them.

"What is it you're sewing?" he asked her after a while.

"It will serve as a curtain for that little window, if I can get it hemmed straight. My embroidery is not very accomplished."

"It looks like a good neat stitch to me."

She had learned her sewing late and poorly, it was a slight

embarrassment to hear him uphold it. She pushed the needle through silently.

"I've sewed up a lot of stirrup leather," he said, "but with a fine needle about all I've done is tie down buttons and darn up little holes."

"Well if you can darn, you can embroider," she said frankly. "Though it may not be any better than mine."

He tipped his head sidewise skeptically. But he said, "That could be. Maybe I just never had anybody show me."

She didn't know if he expected her to make the offer, or hoped she would not.

They were both silent for a while, and then he said, with a slight sound of apology, "I guess this is keeping you from work." It was plain what he meant.

She shook her head once impatiently, without speaking. In spite of the rain, she had planned to make a start today at burning out the stumps, wanting to clear a little of the space given over to garden, now that the potatoes had been dug up and the yellowed vines dug in. But a dying dog shouldn't need his apology.

He watched her. Eventually he said, "You have got a lot done to this place. It was in a bad way when Claud had it."

"Yes."

Perhaps he took that to be ungracious. He didn't say anything more, and her single curt word hung on in the silence.

She said, finally, "I have just got the shed done. I believe I've never worked as hard as I did cutting and notching the logs for that little leanto. I planned to have a fence done by now but the shed has taken so long doing."

He nodded, as if he agreed that, yes, it was hard work cutting logs. Then slowly he said, "You did well by it as far as I could see."

She did not answer that, but she looked over at him and then away. She said, after a silence, "I haven't caulked the walls. I don't know that I will. They'll cut the wind enough as they are, and the roof is tight. A goat will stand the cold better than a cow anyway."

"I guess they will. I've heard that." He let out his slow, wide smile. "Though it may have been you that I heard it from."

She smiled slightly also. "It's true, I defend goats rather more often than I'm asked to."

He gave her a look that was like Mr. Whiteaker's — timid seeming and sideward. "I wonder you didn't buy a place there in Pennsylvania where you were, and commence raising goats in earnest."

She examined the needlework, frowning, while she thought whether or not to answer, and how. Finally, firmly, she said, "I had it in mind to come West and take up ranching." She meant to keep out any sound of childishness, of foolish romanticism, though some of that had inspirited her once.

She could not tell what was in Mr. Odell's look. He kept silent, watching her, as if he thought she would say more. She did, finally, smiling at him deliberately. "The truth is, Mr. Odell, when my husband died I sold every last thing of his just to get the money to come West. I suppose I was seeking the boundless possibilities that are said to live on the frontier." She kept her stiff smile. "I imagine you have never been that foolish."

He looked at her in surprise. He may have misunderstood her. He said, "Tim and me had a friend for a couple of years, Andy Mayes. He got killed, drowned, in a river crossing when we were all working for the Double M up in the Spokane country. Andy had some money saved up in a poke inside his boot, and the boss said we ought to take that, and his gear and his horses too, because he didn't have a family that anybody knew about and we were his friends. So we sold all his stuff and took the poke. We had money of our own we'd saved up, and we put Andy's with it and bought our first cows. The boss let us run our cows with his for a couple of years, and for a few years after that we wrestled with the sheepmen for the free grass over on the plateau. Then we bought up here. But it was Andy's money that got us started."

She saw what he meant by it, that he was offering it to her in a comforting way, perhaps as an ease for guilt. She looked down at her needlework and let the smile go, without an answer.

The dog's wheezing had quieted somewhat but he could not swallow past his swollen throat. When Mr. Odell trickled a little tea down the back of the dog's throat, he retched weakly and the thin green water ran back out the edges of his mouth. Lydia carried on deliberately with the sewing, only watching the dog and the man from an edge of her eye.

The man's face kept its steady look. But in a moment, without looking at Lydia, he said, "I wonder if I shouldn't put him out of the way. I hate to see him suffer this way, and if you say there is nothing you can do for him . . ." He let the words trail off.

"I believe he is bound to die soon," she said. The man's steadiness kept her from too much pity. She felt sober, reasonable, talking with him about the dog's end.

He nodded. "Well," he said. He sat with the dog's head in his lap, one hand resting lightly on the dog's shoulders. Almost as he said the word, the yellow jaws moved, the dog made a long, rattling sound letting out his breath.

They sat and waited, watching the dog. "Well," Mr. Odell said again, when he was sure the dog was dead. Then he said, "If you don't mind, I guess I'll dig a hole for him and just get him buried right here."

"Yes."

He folded the blanket up around the dog's body and carried him out. Lydia stood slowly and put away the needlework and got on her coat and hat. She took the spade and followed the man through the garden, where the kale was all that was left growing among the frost-killed weeds. He had set the dog down on the wet grass at the edge of the worked ground.

"All right?" He looked at her.

"Yes." She handed over the spade.

He dug the hole slowly, keeping the sides straight and piling up the rocky red earth in a neat pyramid. She stood with her hands pushed down in her coat pockets, watching him. The rain had quit for the time being but the air felt wet, and under the trees there was an unsteady showering off the high branches of the evergreens. The bell she had hung on Rose rang an infrequent, timid-sounding note. Otherwise the only sound was the man's huffing breath and the scrape of the spade against the gravelly ground.

Mr. Whiteaker rode his horse up from the end of the clearing while the hole was still being dug. He got down off the horse at a distance and walked up the rest of the way, leaving the horse to stand reins-trailing among the dark stumps. He took up a place on the other side of the hole, opposite to Lydia, without saying a word to either of them. Mr. Odell had looked up once when the horse had first come out of the trees and then he had gone on with digging the hole. Now he said, low, without looking up from what he was doing, "Did you find him?"

Tim Whiteaker shook his head once. "Rain," he said vaguely, and made an irritable gesture with one hand. His face was stiff, his mouth pulled out into the long creases in his cheeks. His eyes were fixed narrowly on the spade, following it back and forth from the hole to the piled-up dirt.

After a while Mr. Odell set the spade aside and knelt on the muddy ground beside the dog's body. He picked up the dog and laid him down in the hole, with the blanket left around him. The shape the dog made under the blanket was indefinite, inanimate. Mr. Odell leaned back and looked at it a moment and then pushed to come standing with a grunt. He began to fill in the hole rapidly, raking in the loose dirt and rocks with the spade. The dirt made a mound when he was done and he tamped it down with the flat of the spade until it looked smooth and hard.

"It was bound to get to this," Tim Whiteaker said after a moment. He spoke in a sort of grumble, bearish and resentful. "It was just luck it didn't happen before now."

She looked at him. He stood with his chin down and his shoulders pulled up so his collar rubbed his hat. The stance had a child's look — as if he stood ready to take a scolding. But there was no boyishness just now in his face, only the bleak look he had worn since walking up to them there at the edge of the garden. A sort of dread came up in her slowly.

"If the poor dogs were poisoned, Mr. Whiteaker, no one would have set out deliberately to do it. It was carelessness. Or mishap." She spoke to him reasonably, watching his face.

It was Blue Odell who looked toward her. Mr. Whiteaker stooped deeper inside his damp coat, not lifting his eyes from the dog's grave. No one spoke. Then Tim said bitterly, "Carelessness is sómething that will get people killed."

She held still, only lifting her chin slightly, drawing up her mouth, against his hardness.

"I don't think Herman's got any pups right now," Mr. Odell said, standing back and then leaning forward slightly on the handle of the spade. "I guess we'll be without dogs for a while." He sounded mild, indifferent, but Lydia saw the look that went between the two men, as if there had been something else said, or some private feeling declared. Left out, or disregarded, she looked away toward the bell goat and the little ribbon of the Jump-Off Creek.

Then Mr. Odell said gently, unexpectedly, "I appreciate what you did to ease the dog, ma'am."

With her mouth still pursed, she answered, "I couldn't do anything to save him."

He shrugged. "I expect there was nothing that could have been done."

After a moment she said, "Perhaps not."

He shifted his weight and then reached the spade toward her. "Thanks."

She nodded. Where she now held the handle of the spade, the heat of the man's hand was still on the wood.

Blue looked over at Tim and then he started out toward his

horse. Tim stood where he was, with his head down looking at the dirt. After a while he made a loose gesture, lifting one hand and turning it, and he shot her a look full of misery. Then he went down after the gray horse. She stayed there at the edge of the garden watching the two of them, with her hands sunk in her pockets. Blue Odell rode his horse back over to where she was. He smiled slowly.

"He's in a testy mood, is all. You shouldn't credit it, ma'am."

She said solemnly, "No. I don't. Thank you, Mr. Odell." Then, bluntly, tipping her head a little to peer at him, she said, "What will you do?"

He looked off toward Mr. Whiteaker who had already started his gray horse down the trail beside the Jump-Off.

"I don't know," he said. "There are two or three wolfers who've been living in a shack kind of above us there, on Loeb's Mountain. We might go up there and talk to them. I expect if we do, we'll ask them to keep their traps and their baits up on the mountain and not come down onto our property anymore. But you shouldn't worry about it, ma'am. One of them we've known a long time, we worked with him up on the Spokane River."

She nodded slowly, seriously. "All right then. I won't worry. Good-by, Mr. Odell."

"So long, ma'am." He touched his hat and started his horse trotting after Tim Whiteaker.

Lydia took the spade and walked across the muddy little garden to the house. She didn't look after the two men until she had come all the way back and stood in the open door. By then, they were at the edge of the clearing, and in the brief moment while she stood watching they went out of sight in the vague shadows under the trees.

# ❋ 34 ❋

It started to rain in earnest, falling straight down in lines thick and dark as pencil strokes. They had come away without any raingear. Tim's coat gradually let the wet through, and the shirt under it grew clammy. He kept his hat pulled down on his ears.

He didn't say anything to Blue, riding up there. But when they got to where they could see Loeb's shack, he stopped his horse. "I haven't seen that kid," Tim said. "I let it drop, the business between him and me." He ducked his head so rain ran off the front of the hat brim in a thin brief sheet. "I didn't want you thinking the dogs were any part of that."

Blue looked over at him. "No," he said. "I figured you would have said, if it was that." He took out his cigarette papers. They were damp, and he fiddled with them a while until he finally got one to come away from the others. "Those fellows don't appear to be at home," he said.

Tim looked up the hill. The shack squatted up there, dark and cold and solitary. There wasn't any smoke drifting up under the overcast. The grass was trampled down, muddy, but no horses stood where he could see.

"I guess I'll go on and look," he said. He started the gray mare on up the hill toward the house. He had his Miller stuck under the fender of the saddle but he didn't pull it out. He could see from here, there wasn't anybody in the shack. When he got up to the yard, he stood off the mare and pulled back the hide that hung in the doorway. Those wolfers were still living in the shack, or somebody was. There were three or four thin blankets on a bed of piled-up dry leaves, and grease had set in a fry pan left on top of the stove. A moldy carcass of a cow with pieces hacked out of it was hung up from a rafter. The place stank of the spoiled meat.

Tim let the door hide fall again and looked back after Blue. The little dun was bringing him up slowly while he smoked his cigarette.

"They left their gear, so I guess they're coming back," he said. He stood close to the house under the narrow eave, out of the rain. "There's a piece of a cow hung up in there," he said after a moment.

Blue sat on the dun in the yard, finishing his cigarette. He was hunched up inside his coat, with his hat pulled down low. He sat stiffly, as if his collarbone was hurting him, but he was maybe just trying to keep his hat level so the rain wouldn't sluice down his back or into his lap.

"There's no telling when they'll be back," he said.

Tim shook his head. "No."

There was a short silence. Blue looked at Tim from under the level hat. "I guess we'll wait for them."

"It's a long ride up here," Tim said, intending it as an answer. Then he said, "I don't know about waiting inside." He wasn't sure why it bothered him to think of waiting in the house.

Blue turned his head carefully, looking off across the bench and down on that fine view. "I don't know," he said vaguely.

They fell silent. There wasn't any other place to get out of the rain up here. Finally Blue bent over and got hold of the gray mare's headstall. He looked at Tim. "I suppose I'd better put the horses down under the trees where they've got some cover." He rode off slowly, leading the gray long-necked behind him.

Tim went inside the shack. He looked at the stove but didn't make a fire. He squatted down on his hips and leaned against a wall, with his forearms resting across his knees. His clothes felt colder, wetter, now that he was inside and out of the rain. He looked at his hands without seeing them.

Blue came in carrying the two rifles. He slid a look at Tim and leaned the Miller gingerly against the wall next to him. He looked around once quickly at the stinking room and then crouched down across from Tim, opposite the door. He stood his own rifle by him and put his hands down between his knees.

Neither of them said anything. Tim chafed his hands together and blew into them and shrugged his shoulders under the wet, clammy coat. The rain quit after a while, but they didn't talk about going outside to wait. Both of them stayed in the house, crouched down silently in the foul-smelling dimness. Tim tried to think about what they were doing, what they would do, but he couldn't stay with it. Everything about it felt slick and gray. It occurred to him that he should have started something in the Dutch pot before they'd left home, so it would be cooked and waiting for them when they got back. He kept thinking of that, and wishing that he'd remembered to do it.

He had taken for granted they'd have a little warning, but they didn't hear anything from outside until a horse snuffled suddenly from close up to the door. A gust of sharp bristling air filled up his chest. He looked at Blue, seeing maybe his own short, startled glance given back in Blue's face. He stood up carefully. His legs were stiff, prickling. He didn't know if he wanted to be holding the rifle when they came in, or not holding it. Finally, without looking at Blue, he picked up the Miller by its breech. He thought about squatting down again. He thought about saying something out loud, letting them know. But he stood dumbly where he was. He knew without looking, that Blue had stood up and not taken hold of his rifle. The kid, Osgood, pushed aside the hide and took a step in. "What!" he said, and his face jerked, going pale and then quickly red when he saw Blue standing there. Then he caught Tim at the edge of his eye and yelled "Shit!" very high and wild, and stumbled backward out the doorway, thrashing his hands against the scabby hide. Tim lurched after him. In his hand a piece of the kid's coat sleeve tore rottenly. He pushed his shoulder past the door hide and fell out in the mud on top of the kid.

The pinto horse skittered sideways away from them and trotted off, his coarse mane whipping out like a flag. The kid hit Tim in the face. There was a rush of red noise and the sky sliding down all at once in front of him. He had a skidding, sideways glimpse of Blue holding the kid by the shirt, and then a gun popped and Blue yelled, "Hey!" and jumped for the shack. Osgood scrambled off the other way. Tim got onto his knees. He hadn't ever let go the rifle. He brought it up and shot at Osgood once, jerkily, as the kid ran away from him down the hill. A little geyser of mud squirted up where the shot hit the ground, way left of Osgood. Farther down the slope a man in a curly sheep's coat rode a buckskin horse down off the bench. He held a carbine out in one hand, sort of brandishing it foolishly, as if he weren't bolting away into the trees. When Tim's shot went off, he jerked around once, but the horse took him on downhill without stopping. When he went out of sight in the trees, he was still holding his rifle out, stiff-armed, and sticking the horse with his spurs. The kid kept running down across the trampled grass alone, his boots slapping clumsily in the mud. Tim heard, all at once, the kid's high, scared, toneless keening. He stared after him. He knelt in the mud, holding the rifle shakily, watching him go.

Afterward, when the kid had gone on down into the trees, he stood up unsteadily and palmed some of the mud off his coat and his knees. He and Blue didn't look at each other, didn't speak. Tim was still shaking a little. He kept brushing at the front of his coat. When blood splashed on his hand, he touched his face in surprise. His mouth was cut, his chin sticky and smeared with blood. He wiped his mouth on his coat sleeve gingerly.

Blue began to make a new cigarette, watching how he did it, his hat shadowing his face. "Shit," he said, low, without lifting his head. Tim looked over at him, across the arm he was holding up to his mouth. Then he looked away. After a while Blue said, "What now?" He was smoking his cigarette, looking down toward the edge of the trees where the two wolfers had gone.

Tim looked there too. "I don't know," he said glumly. Then he said, "Maybe it's over with." Blue looked at him.

They walked down warily off the bench, carrying their rifles. They scouted the edge of the woods. The trees dripped quietly. The prints were a smeared mess, but they found a couple of boot marks going downhill and a long skid in the duff where maybe a horse going down too fast had slipped and then caught itself.

"They went on down, both of them," Tim said.

Blue had hidden the horses out of the way in a little gully below the edge of the trees, holding them there on a peg and a rope. The saddles were wet. They hadn't brought anything to wipe them off with, so they sat on the wet and rode downhill silently in a chilly dusk, holding the rifles in their laps and watching out for the kid and the Montana man without talking about it. After the first couple of hundred feet, Tim never saw any boot marks. He wondered if the Montana man had stopped finally for Osgood and they were both up on the buckskin, or if the kid had gone off the trail, running scared into the brush, or hiding there. Sometimes, Blue hipped around in the saddle and looked back up the trail behind them as if he was thinking about the kid too, but he didn't say anything about it.

Below the mountain, along the little north-running creek, they let the horses have some water. Tim's own mouth was dry, it tasted of blood, but he didn't want to get down off the gray. He felt stiff and achy.

"Danny wasn't with them," Blue said.

Tim looked at him. "No. I guess he wasn't." He didn't know why that made him feel better. Then he knew: he was glad it hadn't been Danny he'd taken that shot at. *Jesus Christ.*

"Maybe he's not wolfing anymore," he said. "They might have split up."

A gun went off, reporting flatly under the wet trees, and both the horses started, throwing up their heads. Blue said, "Oh," in a surprised way, and went down over the shoulder of the dun.

Somebody shot again, splashing up a jet of water, and in the dusk along the hillside Tim saw the little yellow spittle of the gun. He shot at it twice, with the gray jumping under him, before he lost a stirrup and went off clumsily, holding the Miller up high and hitting hard on his hip and his shoulder in the frigid water. He lay there stupidly a moment, out of air, and then grabbed hold of Blue by a pants leg and dragged him out of the water, up under the brush along the edge of the creek.

He squirmed around, getting the rifle up where he could shoot it. He looked at Blue once and then looked at the dark trees and held his breath in, trying to steady his hands. The creek made a small, padded, inoffensive noise running downhill in front of where he lay. That was all he could hear, except his heartbeat booming in his ears. He waited, watching the trees. His chest burned. After a while, after quite a while, Blue made a small sound, a release of air. Tim looked at him. "Blue," he said, starting to cry. Then he looked away. He looked at the horses, trailing their muddy reins, standing high-headed and fidgety a little way down the trail.

When it was dark enough, he crawled out of the brush. He left Blue there and crawled down along the creek in the dark. He sat with his back to a tree and waited, watching the woods and the brushy place where Blue was. He had to keep his teeth clamped down hard on the shivering. A small moon came up but nothing moved in its light except the two horses and the narrow white creek.

When it was daylight he stood up stiffly and waited, standing there, and then he went up the hill. He found Osgood lying on his side in the leaves with his hat squashed up under his head and his hands outspread in front of him holding onto the gun, with the long knobby wrists showing below the cuffs of his too-short jacket. Tim had killed him, shooting wild and scared off the back of the damned horse.

# ❖ 35 ❖

The first day of November was as bright and warm as June but overnight the weather soured and in the morning the sky was black, the ground frozen hard, the wind fierce out of the north-west. Rain began to fall in the afternoon, sleety white, rattling against the frozen ground. The goats and the mule stood under the low roof of the shed, bunched in a close, taciturn flock. On the goats' long dirty fleece, ice hung in peas, hard and filthy. Lydia let them have a few of the yellow squashes she'd put by for these occasions, jealously doling them out by turns. In the lurid twilight she pinched Louise between her knees and let down the milk which froze as it touched the pail, forming a thin bluish crust on the cold tin.

She brought the frozen milk up to the house and thawed it on the stove, Lars's big coat thawing out too while she stood there in it shivering and drinking the milk down hot. The wind hissed through the holes in the house where the cement chinking had cracked and fallen out. It was too cold to do any handwork, or even to write. She heated stones on the stove and took them to bed and pulled the quilts up to cover her head. The frozen rain ticked against the shingles of the roof and gusted up against the walls with a sound like gravel. The black wind racketed in the trees. She pulled the rag rug up off the floor and covered the quilts with it.

When daylight showed between the cracks of the house she unwillingly gave up the bed to get a fire made in the cold stove. There was a heavy rime of ice on the rug and on the stove, frozen puddles on the floor. She laid her clothes on the stove and came back to bed to lie shivering watching them thaw. Afterward, she broke up the ice on the floor, swept it up in a hillock and thawed it in a kettle for the animals. The door was iced shut. She had to kick and pry at it stubbornly until the seal broke and the door swung to let her out.

The freezing rain still fell on the wind. From the eaves of the house and the shed and the privy, ice hung in long white braids. The trees, the stumps were glazed and satiny. The little Jump-Off Creek trickled bare and blackish-looking, caged in ice.

Between the house and the shed the ground was beaten down smooth and the ice overlaid it in a slick, opaque sheet. Her boot soles were worn smooth as the ice. She took a couple of slipping steps and went down sideways, holding the kettle up sloppily level so the water wouldn't be much spilled. Her wrist was cut on the sharp ice, between the edge of her glove and the sleeve of her coat, and she stood again slowly, sucking on it, and then bracing the sore hand on the wall of the house, setting the heels of her boots down watchfully, deliberately, and holding the big kettle low. She went a long way around to the shed, staying close to the brush fence where the uneven ground gave a little better footing. The rain fell slanting and gray, ticking on the brim of her hat, blowing up under it hard and stinging as sand.

She came all the way around slowly to the east end, the open end of the shed, before she saw the caved-in corner of it where the wind had dropped a tree across the back edge of the roof. The logs had slipped down there and the roof had given way, slumping in like old thatch. One of the does, it was Louise, lay dead in the frozen straw at the back of the shed. Rose and her kid and the good steady mule had bolted out, were gone.

She stood holding onto the brittle, icy twigs of the brush fence, staring at this defeat. Then grimly she tipped out the water and carried the empty pail back to the house. She wrapped up her boots in strips of rag, pushed a piece of rope and the mule's bridle down in a pocket of Lars's coat, and went out again.

She went up the clearing along the rough track of the log-drag because they would have gone with the wind behind them. Under the trees, the way was a tangle of downed limbs and windfalls, the brush splayed out with the weight of the ice. She made a deliberate trail through it, tramping on the brittle white branches. She went past the bare tree-cut up the gorge of the Jump-Off. The gully stayed narrow, pinched between the ridges, only widening a little wherever a seasonal creek had cut a trough crosswise to the Jump-Off. She went painstakingly up each of those dead ends, breaking a track through the icy brush and listening for the goat's bell, or whistling for the mule when she could get a sound out of her cold stiff chin, numbed lips.

She had been up this far, fishing the creek, but it was another place now in the white glaze and wreckage of the ice. Limbs broke and fell in a shower whenever the wind gusted, scattering needles and knives of ice. There were countless downed trees as well, and trees still falling intermittently, so that when the wind came up hard she stood in one place and waited, with her shoulders hunched up in a reflex, as if they would take the weight of what might hit her. The rain kept up, blowing along her back. Where her hair straggled out below the hat, it froze to the collar of the gray coat; when she turned her head or bent it down, she heard her hair breaking, as brittle as twigs. There was no track of the mule or the goat under the ice. But she kept the wind behind her and went on doggedly.

The creek divided. She stood at the fork, not able to choose, and then saw the thing lying dead, half in the water, at a distance up the left branch. She stayed where she was, looking at it, blinking her eyelashes against the freezing rain. Then she went up slowly. It wasn't the mule. She had to come right up to it to be sure. It was a thin old cow, black and white, under a skin of ice. The cow's knees were bent under a little, as if she had knelt there first and then tipped over along her side. The carcass was whole, not eaten or cut into. There was no telling what had killed the cow, but no bait had been made of it anyway. Under the scabby ice, the brand had the plain shape of the Half Moon.

Lydia stood in the sleeting wind and stared at the cow. She had kept away from Tim Whiteaker's since Mr. Odell was buried. She had felt a dim fear of calling on him — something not to do with the cruel shootings, but with Mr. Whiteaker's bare and burning look. She didn't know why the old dead cow with his brand on it drove her now suddenly to tears on his account. The tears were cold, few, and straightaway they froze. She had to take a glove off and pick open her icy eyelashes. She peered unhappily along the icebound gully where the cow lay. The wind blew hard, showering ice in a loud, jagged spattering. She pulled up her shoulders until it was done and then determinedly went up the fork of the creek.

She had come away from the house without eating anything, had not even drunk coffee. Hunger was not much of a difficulty, she shut her mind to it. But the narrowing branch of the creek was sealed in ice and she suffered from the want of water. She knew enough not to suck on ice: it deepened the thirst. Twice, she beat through the crust of the creek with a stick and a rock and got a hand down to the water underneath, bringing it up in palmfuls, insufficient, and teeth-aching cold.

Eventually she found the mule. A tree had toppled in some other wind, the weight of it pulling over the root mass intact so the big wheel of dirt and root, in a white glaze of ice, stood high and flat upwind and Rollin was in the dark lee of it with his head down, abject and solitary.

Mules and horses were social, she had never known one who liked to be alone. Rollin, after the other mule was dead, had got to like the company of the goats. Often he trailed Rose in at night, following the bell. Lydia had kept out a little hope they would be found together. So she came up to the mule dourly, as if finding him was the discouragement. She got the bridle out of a coat pocket and put it stiffly on him. Ice had balled in his feet and she hadn't brought a pick, might not have been able to chip his shoes clean anyway. So she didn't get up on his back. She took him by the bridle and led him back downstream — he had come up this way without the goat, or Rose would have been found there with him.

He wasn't happy, facing into the sleet. He pulled his head around stubbornly and stopped, hunching up his hindquarters. She dragged at him and hit him with a stick and finally he came around. She found she had to walk in front of his muzzle, breaking the wind, or every little while he would stop again and try to put his rump to the stinging rain.

The backs of both her hands ached dully. She had been frost-bitten along the backs of her hands once and ever since had been prone to freeze there when the weather was bitter. The gloves she had were sheep's suede with the fleece turned in, they were good gloves but too big for her hands — they had been Lars's. She regularly changed about which hand held the mule's lead, and kept the other one always shoved down in the pocket of Lars's coat. She pulled up the collar of the coat and sank her chin in it and stumped thick-footed through the icy brush. She went by the dead cow without turning her head.

At the fork she turned out of the wind and went up the other branch. Shortly, the way became rocky, narrow, steep. She left the mule with his lead made fast to a tree and kept on a while, climbing up cautiously, holding on to the brush. The rocks were slick, glazed with ice. Finally she stood up straight, gasping air, and looking ahead along the rough steep gorge.

*Damn.* She could not articulate it. Her mouth was dry, her tongue thick and cold.

She peered into the wind, back down the way she had come. The mule stood sullenly with his whiskery muzzle trailing ice in a long white beard.

She climbed down slowly to the mule and stood a moment with her forehead against his cold neck and then she led him bleakly down the gully of the Jump-Off Creek. It was hard, going down against the wind. She kept her chin down, taking the sharp rain on the crown of her hat and stumbling shortsighted with her stare fixed on her boots. Her eyes teared helplessly and the tears froze so that she had to take a glove off every little while to pick the ice from her lashes. Wherever the ground was smooth, the mule was apt to slip on his icy shoes. She undid the rags from her own feet and put them numbly on his. But she was never done with persuading him. She hauled him down the long way home slowly, by fits and starts.

She had to drag the dead goat out from beneath the broken-down corner of the shed roof before the mule would stand under it. Then she tied him there on a stout rope and went in the house. Her hands were stiff. She fumbled, nursing a smoky fire in the stove, and stood over it while ice was melted again in the kettle. Her hands began to burn. She didn't want to go back out in the stinging rain and wind, across the slick field to the shed. But she took hold of the kettle grimly, and clutched a handful of precious sheaf oats in her other hand, and shoved the door back with her hip.

The mule pushed his nose down in the water. She pulled his head up after a moment and numbly walked him back and forth along the front edge of the shed. Then she let him drink again loudly, bumping his muzzle against the bottom of the kettle in his nervous thirst. Lydia heard a scrabble on the ice and looked. Rose led her kid out of the brush, coming anxiously across the field for the water. The clapper of the bell was frozen, but on the goat's long fleece hard marbles of ice rattled flatly. Lydia stood and looked, with her hands in her coat pockets and her shoulders hunched up coldly.

Rose came in under the edge of the shed and pushed her face down eagerly in the kettle. The mule had begun to snuffle the sheaf oats by then, and the goat licked the cold tin with her tongue and blatted and pushed the empty kettle around. She wouldn't stand still for the kid, trying to get at her teat. Lydia looked at her, without the energy for feeling. She took the piece of rope out of her coat. It was stiff, rimed with ice. She put it around the doe's neck and tied the end around one of the poles of the shed. Her fingers worked the knots poorly, laboriously. Crossing the field with the empty kettle, she fell on the ice and sat there crying dryly, tiredly. But she got up after a while and went on the rest of the way, because the goat was bawling, thirsty, waiting for her.

✸ **36** ✸

*11 Dec* Bright today and cold, the old Snow under the trees & on the North sides of the ridges frozen hard. Went over in the Morning to Mr Whiteaker's with potatoes & a squash and had a Visit, tho I had dreaded it and put off going rather longer than was kind. The missing Dog of his has come meekly home, no telling where he had been or if the other was poisoned after all. Mike Walker had told me Mr Whiteaker was brooding over this, imagining events might have ended differently if the Dog had been found on the Day. But he keeps the Dog in the house w him, it may be as company against Loneliness, and I believe he does not hold the poor dog to account, no more than Fate. We had a good talk once started, comprising of the prospects for more Snow & of our supplies holding out & sick Cows & Mrs Walker's successful delivery of a Son. He said the Jump-Off Creek was named due to the Whitman party camping along it in 1837 on their way to starting the mission at Waiilatpu, it was the "jump-off point" for crossing the Summit of the Blue Mts & down onto

the Walla Walla plain. I was rather foolishly happy when I heard
it, as Narcissa Whitman & Eliza Spalding in that Party were the
first White Women to cross the Continent and I believe I felt
some kinship w them. On account of our speaking of names, I
got up courage & deliberately asked him if Mr. Odell was named
for the Blue Mts or if it was part of a longer Indian naming. He
was not unhappy w my raising the name of the dead, it could be
he was glad for it. He said No & told a long story about a near-
drowning in a frozen lake & Mr Odell brought up blue as block-
ice, thought to be dead, and when left in a cold room he came
Awake & afterwards always was called Blue. His true given name,
which not many knew, was Lincoln, after the President. He had
rather less Indian about him than seemed. We had a talk about
putting up Hay, Mr Whiteaker more disposed to it than before-
time. When I said I had made Hay, he said he would learn it
from me if I would teach him, and I said I would.

## About the Author

Author photograph © Gretchen Corbett

Molly Gloss is the author of several novels including *The Jump-Off Creek*, *The Dazzle of Day*, *Wild Life*, *The Hearts of Horses*, and *Falling from Horses*, as well as the story collection *Unforeseen*. Her work has received, among other honors, a PEN West Fiction Prize, an Oregon Book Award, two Pacific Northwest Booksellers Awards, the James Tiptree Jr. Award, and a Whiting Writers Award. A fourth-generation Oregonian, she lives in Portland.

# Novels by Molly Gloss

*from*

HARPER ⬤ PERENNIAL

### A PEN/Faulkner Award Finalist

"Drawing on pioneer diaries, journals and hand-me-down stories of her own ancestors, Gloss displays a deep awareness not only of the brutal hardships of frontier life, but also of the moral codes and emotional attachments of the people who settled there." —*Publishers Weekly*

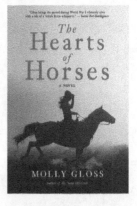

"Magnificent . . . Molly Gloss has brilliantly recreated a bygone time and place."
—**Howard Frank Mosher,**
author of *On Kingdom Mountain*

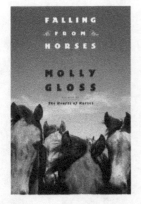

"The story of a boy growing up into a man by way of ambition, adventure, catastrophe, love, and grief. A beautiful, moving novel, cut from the American heartwood."
—**Ursula K. Le Guin,** author of *Lavinia* and *The Unreal and the Real: Selected Stories*